I0649612

Stalked By Magic

Stalked By Magic

BY

TRACY WILSON

http://beautifulpublications.com

Published by
Beautiful Publications LLC
Stratford, CT 06614

This book is a work of fiction. Names, characters, places, and incidents are either products of the author's imagination or are used fictitiously. Any resemblance to actual events or locales or persons, living or dead, is entirely coincidental.

©Copyright 2022 Tracy Wilson

All rights reserved. No part of this publication may be reproduced or transmitted in any form or by any means, electronic or mechanical, including photocopy, recording, or any information storage and retrieval system, without permission in writing from the copyright owner, except by a reviewer who may quote brief passages in a review.

LIBRARY OF CONGRESS CONTROL NUMBER:
2022909617

PRINT ISBN: 979-8-9855290-5-0
EBOOK ISBN: 979-8-9855290-4-3

Printed in the United States of America

Disclaimer

This is **NOT** a novel about the NBA player, Earvin 'Magic' Johnson.

PROLOGUE

"That's her..."

"Oh damn – now I see why you've been so pre-occupied..."

"I'm about to go in..." Jake said as he got up and started walking towards her...

"Magic – wait!!" Leonard exclaimed as he got up...

"What?!"

"Le'me get the other one..."

"Fine – let's go – she's about to get away!" Jake exclaimed as they hurried over towards the concession stand...

CHAPTER 1

"FUUCCCKKK!!" Lina exclaimed as the drink fell out of her hand...

"I'm sorry..." Jake said as he turned his head..."

"I can't believe we stood in line for 20 minutes for nothing..." Bri sighed...

"I'm sorry – I'll buy you another one – Sir – please give her another drink..." Jake said as he handed the casher a $20..."

"Thank you..." Lina said...

"Can I buy you a drink?" Leonard asked Bri as he smiled...

"You have a nice smile..." Bri sighed...

"Hello! People are waiting and halftime's almost over!" Someone yelled from the back of the line...

"Here – give her whatever she wants..." Leonard said as he handed the cashier a $20...

"What if I want your phone number?" Bri asked...

"Oh my God – will you hurry up?!" someone yelled from the back of the line...

"Here ya go ladies..." the cashier said as he handed Lina a tray with two drinks...

"I'll walk you back to your seat..." Jake said...

"Where are you sitting?" Bri asked...

"We're sitting down there..." Leonard answered as he pointed out where they were sitting...

"Nice seats – we're sitting way up there..." Lina sighed...

"Come with us..." Jake said as he took the tray in one hand and took Lina's hand with the other...

"We don't have tickets for those seats..." Lina sighed...

"Don't worry about it – the Knicks are losing – people always leave at halftime..."

"You sure?" Bri asked...

"We're sure..." Leonard answered as he took Bri's hand and they headed down towards the better seats...

"What if they come check?" Bri asked as they sat down...

"They never check..." Jake answered...

"I'm Bri..." Bri sighed as she smiled at Leonard...

"I'm Leonard..." he said as he kissed her hand... "But you can call me Len..."

"Nice to meet you Len..."

"Give me your phone..."

"Okay." Bri watched as he put his number in her phone... "Who are you calling?"

"I'm calling myself..."

"Why are you calling yourself?" she laughed...

"So I can get your number too..."

"You would've gotten my number when I called you..." she laughed...

"Yes!" Lina exclaimed as Kobe hit a 3-pointer...

"Is he your favorite?" Jake asked...

"Yea – well him and Pau Gasol..."

"I like him too..."

"I see you're wearing Magic's number..."

"My father gave this to me..."

"My father doesn't even like basketball!" Lina laughed...

"I'm really sorry about earlier..."

"That's okay – besides – you bought me another..." she laughed...

"Nice meeting you Me..." Jake laughed...

"I'm Lina..."

"I'm Jake – but my friends call me Magic..."

"Because of the jersey?" Jake got really quiet. Lina noticed a change in his demeanor and became concerned... "Are you okay?" she asked as she touched his hand...

"Yea..." he sighed...

"You wanna talk about it?"

"Let's just watch the game..."

"Okay..." Leonard smiled to himself as he took Bri's hand. Bri thought he was smiling at her but Leonard was actually smiling at the fact that Jake had Lina right where he wanted her...

"Tacos!!" Lina and Bri exclaimed as the Lakers scored 100 points...

"You want tacos?" Leonard asked...

"I love tacos – but I don't love 'em enough to stand in line for 30 minutes just for them to tell us they ran out..." Bri laughed...

"I'll take you to El Cholo if you want tacos..."

"We love El Cholo!" Bri exclaimed...

"Jake – are you okay?" Lina asked...

"I'm okay – I'm just thinking..." he sighed...

"Looks like the game's about to be over – you wanna head out now?" Leonard asked as he leaned behind Bri's shoulder to talk to Jake...

"Can we wait?" Lina asked...

"We can wait if you want..." Jake answered...

"I hate being in the middle of the crowd trying to get out..." Lina said...

"I hope El Cholo is still open..." Bri sighed...

"You don't have to worry about that – it's Friday night – we're good..." Leonard said...

"How long do they stay open?"

"As long as they have customers – especially on Fridays..." Lina sat quiet and watched Jake intently as the crowd began to dissipate...

"We good to go now?" Jake asked...

"We can go now..." Lina answered. They all got up and went upstairs towards the concession stand...

"Le'me go to the bathroom right quick..." Leonard said as he grabbed Bri by the hand, pulled her into the men's room, and locked the door...

"Oh hell no – open this damn door!!" Lina yelled as she began banging on the door...

"I'm alright Lina!" Bri laughed...

"You sure?"

"I'm fine..."

"What kind of guys do you think we are?" Jake laughed...

"I'm sorry – I saw him pull her in there – I heard the door lock..."

"I'll be sure to remember that..." he laughed...

"C'mere..." Leonard whispered as he took Bri's hand...

"No – do what you need to do so we can get outta here!" she laughed...

"I said c'mere..." he whispered as he pulled her close to him and held her...

"Jake?"

"Call me Magic – they call me Jake all day at work...

"What's wrong?"

"You asked me if they call me Magic because of my father's jersey earlier..."

"I'm sorry – I didn't mean to upset you..."

"Leonard... Stop..." Bri breathed in between kisses...

"You don't want me to stop..." he breathed as he kissed her harder...

"You're right..." she breathed as she kissed him back... "But I need you to stop..."

"Okay..." he breathed as he moved her hand down to his dick and rubbed her hand up and down on his crotch... "I'll stop..." Bri's chest was heaving up and down as he backed away from her. Leonard unbuckled his pants slowly, slid his pants and boxers down off his ass, and turned to face her so she could see his dick. After he turned towards the urinal, he smiled to himself...

"My grandfather named my father Jake Magic. My father named me Jake Magic..."

"Is that why they call you Magic?"

"My father took me to all the Laker games when I was little. He told me my grandfather took him to Laker games when he was little. My grandfather went to all the Laker games when they were in Minneapolis..."

"Minneapolis?"

"Yea. The Lakers were in Minneapolis for 13 years. They moved to Los Angeles in 1960. My grandfather moved to Los Angeles right after the Lakers did so he could be near them. He was so happy when Magic joined the team. Magic became his favorite player so when my father was born, he was named Jake after my grandfather and Magic after Magic..."

"Wow! I never knew the Lakers were in Minneapolis!"

"I didn't either...."

"You said was..."

"My grandfather died 10 years ago..."

"I'm sorry..."

"Thank you..."

"What about your dad?"

"He died two years ago..."

"Oh Magic..." Lina said as she pulled him into a hug and held him...

"I can't believe I'm doing this..." Bri breathed as Leonard eased himself inside her...

"Damn..." he moaned in her ear as she pulled him in deeper...

"I still miss him..." Jake sighed...

"I know..."

"I'm sorry... it's just..." Lina kissed him before he could finish...

"We're ready..." Leonard announced as they walked up on Lina and Jake kissing...
"Let's go – I'm hungry..." Lina said...
"You ladies go ahead – we'll be right behind you..." Jake said as he looked over at Leonard...

"You're such a slut..." Lina laughed...
"I couldn't help it!" Bri laughed...
"Sure you couldn't..." Lina teased as she pushed the button for the elevator...
"Once I saw it... I couldn't resist..."
"Was it good?"
"Hell yea!"

"Mission accomplished?" Jake asked...
"Mission Accomplished!" Leonard exclaimed...
"Are you gonna ghost this one too?"
"Naa – I might marry her..."
"Oh shit! Le'me find out!"
"She ain't had none in a while..."
"How you know that?"
"Cause I bust that pussy open!" he laughed...
"Be quiet!" Jake snapped before they got to the elevator...

"Is El Cholo still open?" Bri asked as they got in the elevator...
"I gotchu – don't worry..." Leonard answered. When they got downstairs a black limousine pulled up in front of the Staples Center...
"Ladies – that's our ride..." Jake said...

8

"Okay!" they squealed as they ran towards the limo...

"You didn't tell me you were calling your driver..." Leonard said...

"You volunteered tacos..."

"You didn't wanna go out?"

"You know what happens at El Cholo..."

"I know what happens to you at El Cholo..." Leonard laughed as they got to the limo...

"What happens at El Cholo?" Lina asked as Jake opened the door for them...

"I get drunk..." Jake laughed as he got in and closed the door...

"El Cholo Sir?" the driver asked...

"What I tell you about calling me Sir?"

"I'm sorry Sir – I mean Mr. Jake Sir – I mean..."

"Dan?" Jake interrupted...

"Yes Sir?"

"Never mind..." he laughed as Leonard, Bri, and Lina laughed along with him...

"Shall I wait here for you S.. – Mr. Jake?"

"Yes Dan..."

"Very well..." Jake opened the door, got out, and held the door open as Lina got out, followed by Bri and Leonard...

"Let's go eat some tacos..." he said as they walked towards the restaurant...

"Magic! Leonard! Good to see you!" the manager greeted...

"Good to see you too John..." Jake said...

"Hey..." Leonard greeted...

"Table for four – here's a nice table – follow me..." John said as he picked up the menus...

"You must come here a lot..." Lina said...

"I don't come here that much – he was a good friend of my father..." The waitress was waiting when they got to the table...

"Can I start you off with some drinks?"

"I'll have the El Cholo Margarita!" Bri exclaimed...

"Make it two..." Lina said...

"I'll have the Patron Platinum..." Leonard said...

"And a Herradura Suprema for you – right?" she asked Jake...

"Right..."

"I'll be right back..." she said as she went to place the order...

"Good thing you're not driving!" Lina laughed...

"Oh so you know about the Herradura Suprema..." Jake said...

"I sure do... and I'll never drink it again..."

"You must'a got twisted..."

"Something like that..." Lina sighed. There was an awkward silence before Bri spoke...

"Hey – let's share a Fiesta Platter..."

"I thought you wanted tacos?" Leonard asked...

"I did – but the Fiesta Platter looks really good..."

"Okay – Fiesta Platter for 2..."

"Fiesta Platter for 4..."

"How do you know they want that?" Leonard laughed...

"It's not for them!" Bri laughed...

"Oh – okay!" Leonard laughed...

"I'll have the Filet Mignon Tacos..." Lina said...

"I'ma have the Enchiladas Mariscos with a side of yellow rice & beans..." Jake said as the waitress came back with the drinks...

"Here you go..." she said as she put the drinks on the table... "Will you be having your Filet Mignon Tacos tonight Magic?"

"No – but my lady will..." he answered as he put his arm around Lina...

"You make a nice couple..."

"Thank you..."

"So what can I get you Magic?"

I'll have the enchiladas Mariscos with a side of yellow rice & beans..."

"Got it – what can I get for you?" she asked Bri...

"We'll have the Fiesta Platter..."

"Will that be for 2 or 4?"

"Four..." Bri and Leonard answered in unison and then they bust out laughing...

"I'll be right back..." she said as she went to place the order...

"Here's to happy couples..." Leonard said as he raised his drink...

"I know that's right!" Bri exclaimed as she raised her drink...

"To happy couples..." Jake said as he raised his drink...

"Happy couples..." Lina sighed as she raised her drink...

"Oh damn – this is good!" Bri exclaimed as she gulped her drink down...

"Easy Bri – I need you to get some food in your stomach first..." Leonard said...

"I'll be alright – besides – if I can't walk – you'll carry me!" she laughed...

"I sure hope you're hungry!" the waitress said as she set the tray beside the table...

"Ooohhh – maybe I should'a got that!" Lina exclaimed as she looked at Bri and Leonard's food...

"Oh shit – those tacos look good!" Bri exclaimed as the waitress put them on the table...

"Here you go Magic..." she said as she put his food on the table...

"Bless this food – Amen!" Lina exclaimed as she picked up a taco...

"Amen!" they all said in unison...

"Anybody need a refill?" the waitress asked...

"Me!" Bri exclaimed...

"Coming right up..." the waitress said as she went to get Bri another drink...

"You good?" Jake asked Lina...

"Mmm Hmmm..." she answered as she chewed and they all laughed...

"Here's your refill – anybody else need a refill?" the waitress asked...

"Naa... we're good..." Leonard answered. Lina and Jake were so into each other they didn't realize Leonard and Bri were finished eating...

"Ready when you are..." Leonard said...

"I'm not rushing..." Jake laughed...

"My bad – take your time..." he said as he put his arm around Bri...

"Here's your order to go..." the waitress said as she put a bag on the table...

"Thank you Maria..." Jake said...

"You're welcome – here's your check...

"Put it on my tab..."

"Okay Magic – nice to see you again – congratulations – good night..." she said as she walked away from them and went to another table...

"Why is she congratulating you?" Lina asked...

"Because I told her you're my lady..."

"Ooohhh..."

"C'mon Bri..." Leonard laughed as he helped her up from the table. When they got outside Jake opened the door for them to get in. After they all got in, Jake got in and then he passed the bag up to Dan...

"Thank you Jake..."

"You're welcome..."

"Where to?"

"We live a few blocks from here..." Bri slurred...

"Straight ahead..." Lina said. They rode in silence as Bri fell asleep on Leonard's shoulder... "We're at the corner right there..." After Dan pulled over, Leonard tried to wake Bri...

"Bri..."

"Huh?"

"We're home..."

"Aww..."

"What's wrong?"

"You said we're home..." she sighed...

"C'mon – I'ma help you upstairs..." Leonard said as he tried to move Bri...

"Le'me get the door for you Sir..." Dan said..

"Thank you Dan..." Leonard said as Dan opened the door...

"C'mon Lina..." Jake said as he extended his hand to help her out the limo... "I'll be back in a few Dan..."

"Take your time..." Dan said as he tore into the bag...

"Good night y'all..." Bri slurred as Leonard walked her around the corner...

"I'ma walk you to your door..." Jake said...

"That's okay... we can just say good night right here..."

14

"What's wrong?"

"Nothing..."

"I'm walking you to your door..."

"You don't have too – I'm fine..."

"No you're not..." Jake said as he held the door open for her. Lina went inside and he followed her up the steps to her door...

"This is it..." Bri slurred as she took out her keys...

"Le'me help you with that..." Leonard said as he took the keys from her, put the key in the lock and unlocked her door...

"You wanna come in?"

"You sure?"

"Get in here!" she laughed as she pulled him inside...

"Can we talk?" Jake asked...

"Sure..." Lina sighed...

"Inside?"

"I guess..." she sighed as she unlocked her door and opened it...

"You have a nice place..."

"I'm not ready..."

"I know..."

"You know?"

"Let's talk..." he said as he took her hand and led her into the living room and they sat on the sofa...

"Fuck me..." Bri moaned...

"Is this whatchu want?"

"Yes... Huh..."

"Uggh! Uggh! Uggh!"

"Huh! Huh! Huh!"

"Uggh! Uggh! Uggh! UGGH! UGGH!"

"Haa... Haa... Haa... HAA... HAAA!!"

"Damn that was good!" Leonard breathed as he rolled over on his back... "Where's the bathroom?"

"Down... the... hall..." Bri yawned...

"I'll be right back..." he said as he got up...

"What happened?" Jake asked as he took Lina's hand...

"I don't wanna talk about it..." she answered as she looked away from him...

"Look at me Lina..." Lina looked at him with tears in her eyes...

"I wanted to try that drink..."

"Oh my God... somebody hurt you..." Jake whispered as he wrapped his arm around her...

"I got really drunk... that doesn't usually happen... that never happens..."

"Who?"

"I don't know his name... but I'll never forget him..."

"I'm sorry Lina..."

"I didn't know he put something in my drink until I went to the hospital..."

"Hospital?"

"We had tacos... he told me to try that drink... he said it was really good... I drank it... and..."

"What happened?"

"I woke up in the hospital..."

"So you don't remember what happened?"

"The doctor said they called an ambulance because I passed out..."

"At the restaurant?"

"Yea..."

"So he didn't take you home?"

"No..."

"But he wanted to..."

"The doctor told me they found Rohypnol, GHB (liquid ecstasy), and Ketamine (Special K) in my blood..." Lina whispered as she started crying...

"A date rape cocktail..." Jake confirmed...

"It's my fault..."

"Don't ever let me hear you say that again..." he said as he put his hand under her chin, lifted her head up, and looked in her eyes...

"I'm sorry... I..." Jake interrupted her with a kiss...

"Well shit..." Leonard sighed as he came back into the bedroom. Bri was snoring on her back with her mouth open... "Oh well – I might as well get some sleep – I'ma have fun explaining this tomorrow..." he said as he picked up his phone, sent Jake a text, put the phone down, and climbed into bed beside Bri...

"Hold on a sec..." Jake said as he felt his phone vibrate in his pocket. He took his phone out his pocket and read the message... "Leonard's spending the night..."

"Oohh..."

"I'ma get ready to go..."

"Bri doesn't know..."

"She doesn't?"

"She thinks I had alcohol poisoning from drinking too much..."

"You two are close?"

"Yea..."

"But you don't wanna tell her..."

"No..."

"I won't tell her... or Leonard..."

"Thank you..." she said as she kissed him...

"I need you to do something for me..."

"What?"

"Give me your phone..."

"Here..." Jake put his number in her phone, saved it under Magic, and gave it back to her...

"I want you to call me if you ever see him again..."

"Can I call you for anything else?"

"You can call me for anything you want..."

"Anything?"

"Anything..."

"Okay..." she sighed as she smiled...

"I like that..."

"What?"

"You're smiling..." he said as he gave her a quick kiss and then he left...

CHAPTER 3

"Aaah!!" Bri screamed...

"Wha... What's wrong?" Leonard yawned...

"What the hell are you doing here?"

"You don't remember what happened last night?" he asked as he propped himself up on his elbow...

"I wasn't that drunk..." she sighed...

"So you do remember..."

"Yea..."

"So... do you think last night was a mistake?"

"Honestly?"

"Yea – be honest..."

"I didn't think you'd be here..."

"You deserve better than that..."

"I know... I just..."

"C'mere..." he whispered as he pulled her into a kiss...

"I'm not used to this..."

"You're not used to morning sex?" he breathed as he pushed her down on her back...

"Len... don't..."

"You want me to stop?"

"Yea..." she sighed as she got up out of the bed...

"You want me to leave?"

"No..." she answered as she took her robe off the back of the bedroom door, put it on, and went to the bathroom...

"What the fuck is happening..." Leonard sighed as he sat up, reached for his pants, and began getting dressed...

"Hey Lina..." Jake answered...

"How'd you know it was me?"

"I don't get spam calls at this hour..." he laughed...

"You still get spam calls?"

"Yea..."

"Me too – they come up as Scam Likely!" she laughed...

"How was your night?"

"It was okay..."

"Just okay?"

"I couldn't sleep..."

"I should've stayed..."

"Then we both would've been up all night..."

"Is that right?"

"That's not what I meant!" she laughed...

"What did you mean then?"

"We would've been talking..."

"All night?"

"Yea..."

"Naa – I'da fell asleep on your ass!" he laughed...

"On my ass huh?"
"Now see – you startin' trouble..."
"Sorry..."
"You don't need to apologize..."
"Thanks..."
"For what?"
"Last night..."
"You're welcome..."
"Can you come get me?"
"I'm on my way..."

"Smells good..." Leonard said as he came into the kitchen...
"Sit down – I'll make you a cup..."
"Okay..." Leonard sat at the table and watched Bri take two mugs down from the cabinet...
"How do you like your coffee?"
"Black and strong..."
"So you like it like you then..." she said as she put a mug of coffee in front of him...
"So you think I'm strong then..." he said as she put cream and sugar in her coffee...
"I know you are..." she answered as she sat down at the table with him...
"Well then..." he said as he sipped his coffee...
"How's your coffee?"
"It's good..."
"Glad you like it..."
"So are we going to talk about last night?"
"I've never done that before..."
"Never?"
"Never..."
"So I was your first?"
"Yea..."

"I'm humbled..."

"Really?"

"Why me?"

"Cause I'm feelin' you..."

"I'm feelin' you too..."

"You wanna go out to breakfast?"

"Can we have dessert first?"

"Meet me in the shower..." Bri answered as she stood up, opened her robe, and started walking towards the bathroom...

"Good morning..." Jake said as he lowered the window...

"Good morning! This is nice!" Lina exclaimed as she admired his yellow corvette stingray...

"Thank you..."

"How do I open the door?"

"You don't..." he answered as he got out the car and went to open the door for her...

"Oh wow!" she exclaimed as she got in. Jake closed the door, went over to the driver's side, opened the door, and got in...

"Can I ask you something?" she asked as he started the car...

"You just did..." he laughed...

"Can I ask you something else?"

"You just did!" he laughed again...

"So... after you left last night... I couldn't sleep..."

"Okay..."

"So I googled you – I mean – I googled Magic Johnson..."

"Why?"

"Are you upset with me?"

"No – I'm just curious..."

"You told me all about your grandfather and your father so I wanted to look it up..."

"Me? Or the Lakers?"

"The Lakers!" she laughed...

"Really?"

"I saw something else too..."

"Oh yea?"

"Yes – I saw your name is a variant of Jack and a medieval diminutive of John..."

"So I'm evil?" he laughed...

"No – John originates in Hebrew and means God is merciful..."

"Is that right..."

"I looked up your personality too..."

"My personality?"

"According to Google, people with your name are perceived as someone who is full of life, uplifting, inspiring, and charming..."

"That would be me..."

"I can't wait to tell Bri what I found out about my man..."

"Did you just say your man?"

"Yea..." Lina sighed as she took Jake's hand in hers and his phone started ringing...

"Yo!" he answered...

"What's good?" Leonard asked...

"You tell me..."

"Bri wants breakfast..."

"So do I" Lina exclaimed...

"Hey Lina!" Bri exclaimed...

"Hey Bri!"

"I'll meet you at the Pantry Café..." Leonard said...

"See you in a few...." Jake said as he hung up...

"Do we still have time for breakfast?" Lina asked..."

"They serve breakfast until 1 p.m...."

"Good – 'cause I'm hungry..."

"You know they have other food there besides breakfast – right?"

"Yes – but I want breakfast – and coffee..." she laughed...

"You get cranky when you don't have coffee – don't you?"

"I'm sorry..."

"You don't need to apologize – I'll just make sure I remember that..." he laughed as they pulled up in front of the restaurant...

"Bri!" Lina exclaimed as they ran towards each other..."

"Lina!" Bri exclaimed as they hugged...

"Didn't they just see each other last night?" Jake asked Leonard...

"I guess this is what we have to look forward too..." Leonard laughed...

"Lina – go ahead and get a table – I need to talk to Len for a sec..."

"C'mon Bri!" Lina exclaimed as she grabbed Bri's hand and pulled her inside...

"Good morning – table for two?" the hostess asked...

"Table for four..." Lina answered...

"There's going to be a 30-minite wait..."

"That's fine..."

"That's fine?!" Bri exclaimed...

"That's fine..." Lina repeated...

"Name for reservation please..."

"Lina..."

"We'll call you when your table's ready – next!"

"So how was your night?" Jake asked Leonard...

"It was aiight..."

"Just aiight?"

"Round one was great..."

"What happened?"

"I went to the bathroom and when I got back – she was snoring..."

"Oh – you wanted some more pussy..." Jake laughed...

"Yea..."

"Why'd you stay?"

"Cause I wanted to..."

"You're really feelin' her..." Jake said as he smiled...

"Yea..."

"I'm happy for you – I just hope she's feelin' you too..."

"She is..."

"You sure about that?"

"She asked me how I like my coffee..."

"Oh wow..." Jake said sarcastically...

"I told her I like it black & strong and she says oh so you like it like you then..."

"Oh shit – okay – I see you!"

"It gets better..."

"I'm listening..."

"She told me I was her first..."

"She was a virgin?"

"Naa... she wasn't a virgin..."

"Oh – whew!"

"I would've never took her in the bathroom if she was a virgin..."

"Really? Where would have taken her then?"

"I would've taken her home..."

"And then you would've took her at home!" Jake laughed...

"You're right!" Leonard laughed...

"So did you get any pussy this morning?"

"Damn you nosey!" Leonard laughed...

"Well?"

"We drank coffee, she told me she was feelin' me, she asked me if I wanted to go out to breakfast... and then she told me to meet her in the shower for dessert!"

"Damn – sometimes I wish I could be you..." Jake sighed...

"Aww damn! You didn't get any pussy?"

"I didn't stalk her to get pussy – I stalked her to get close to her..."

"Okay – who are you and where is my friend Magic?"

"I want her – I wanted her – but she's not ready..."

"She's a virgin?!"

"I don't think so..."

"What happened?"

"She didn't want me to walk her to her door – she wanted to say good night and go upstairs by herself..."

"Oh damn – that's cold..."

"I convinced her to let me upstairs. She let me in and we talked. That's when she told me she wasn't ready – but I already knew that..."

"Damn – she's been through some shit..."

"Yea..."

"Did she talk about it?"

"I was still with her when you text me..."

"Okay – you got her to open up to you – you got her to trust you..."

"Yea..."

"And you didn't make a move?"

"Nope..."

"You're a good man Magic..."

"I know..."

"Shut up!" Leonard laughed...

"So how was your night?" Lina asked...

"It was great..."

"You're such a slut!" Lina laughed...

"Do you really think I'm a slut?"

"No!"

"Stop calling me that then..."

"Sometimes I wish I could be more like you..."

"Really? Why?"

"You're not afraid to take chances..."

"I never told you that!"

"So you are afraid?"

"I screamed when I woke up this morning..."

"Why?"

"Because Leonard was there..."

"Isn't that what you wanted?"

"It's what I've always wanted..."

"I don't get it..."

"He stayed..." she whispered as she started crying...

"Bri no... Don't cry..."

"No one ever stayed..."

"Ooohhh – now I get it..."

"I was drunk – he had his way with me – and he still wanted to be with me – he wanted to have sex again this morning – I wanted to – but I stopped him..."

"Why?"

"I didn't want to get caught up if he wasn't really feelin' me..."

"Well he's here so obviously he's feelin' you..."

"Yea – he's feelin' me... and I'm feelin' him too – we talked about it over coffee..."

"You had coffee? I wish I had some coffee earlier..."

"So how was your night?"

"It wasn't..." Lina sighed...

"Oh no – what happened?"

"I didn't want him to come upstairs but..."

"Wait a minute – you two were really into each other at El Cholo..."

"That's why I didn't want him to come upstairs..."

"You didn't want to lead him on..."

"That's not the only reason..."

"Lina – what's going on?"

"I need to tell you something..."

"Lina – you're scaring me..."

"You remember the night I got drunk at El Cholo and I wound up in the hospital?"

"Yea – you had alcohol poisoning – you drank too much..."

"That's not what happened..."

"What happened?"

"I only had one drink..."

"You passed out..."

"I was drugged..."

"You were drugged? He drugged you?"

"Yea..." Lina answered with tears in her eyes...

"Oh my God – why didn't you tell me?"

"I was embarrassed..."

"Why? It wasn't your fault!"

"I wanted to be with him – he didn't have to do that..."

"So that's why you didn't want Jake to come upstairs..."

"I told him I wasn't ready – he said he knew..."

"Aww... that's sweet... wait a minute – what happened last night?"

"We talked... I cried... he comforted me... and then he went home..." Lina sighed...

"You wanted him to stay – didn't you?"

"I'm so confused..." Lina sighed...

"Lina – party of four – your table's ready..."

"I was just about to go outside and get you..." Bri said as Leonard and Jake walked inside...

"Perfect timing..." Lina said...

"Follow me!" the hostess said as she grabbed four menus. When they got to the table there was a pot of coffee waiting for them...

"Oh thank God!" Lina exclaimed as she sat down and made herself a cup of coffee with hazelnut creamer and started sipping it...

"Thank God you got some coffee..." Jake laughed as he sat down next to her...

"Was I that bad?"

"You weren't bad..."

"What can I getcha?" the waitress asked...

"I'll have the #3 – sausage, scrambled, potatoes, and French toast!" Lina exclaimed...

"That sounds good – I want that too!" Bri exclaimed...

"I'll have the steak & eggs..." Jake said...

"I'll have the pork chops & eggs... Leonard said...

"You got it!" the waitress said as she walked away to place their orders...

"Anybody else want coffee?" Lina asked...

"Might as well..." Leonard answered. Lina poured them all a cup of coffee and poured another one for herself...

"Oh good – they have French vanilla..." Bri said as she opened the creamer...

"Do we have enough hazelnut?" Jake asked...

"They have eight left – that's enough for us..." Lina answered as the waitress came back to the table with their food...

"Breakfast is served..." she said as she placed their food on the table...

"Thank you..." Bri said...

"You're welcome – here's your check..." the waitress said as she placed it on the table...

"Uh huh – I asked you out to breakfast..." Bri said as she picked up the check before Leonard could...

"Thank you Bri..." he said...

"Le'me give you something towards the check..." Jake said...

"I got it..." Bri said...

"Okay then..."

"So what are we doing after we leave here?" Lina asked as everyone started eating...

"What would you like to do?" Jake asked...

"I'd like to spend the day with you..."

"Okay..."

"I have to work this afternoon..." Leonard said...

"On Saturday?" Bri asked...

"I'm the Research Program Administrator for Networking & Cyber Security at the USC Vertibi School of Engineering – I normally work Monday through Friday but we all rotate Saturdays – today's my Saturday..."

"I'm the Front Desk Manager at the Courtyard Marriott downtown – I work Monday through Friday – the Assistant Manager works on the weekends..." Bri said...

"I'm the Administrator Assistant at Adams & Martin..." Lina said...

"The law firm?" Jake asked...

"The law firm..." Lina confirmed...

"What the difference between an administrative assistant and an administrator assistant?" Bri asked...

"More work..." Lina laughed...

"I'm a Principal Technology Analyst for the Superior Court..." Jake said...

"So you manage all the computers?" Lina asked...

"I partner with the managers..."

"I guess I'll be going back home after breakfast..." Bri sighed...

"That's a good thing..." Leonard said...

"Why is that a good thing?"

"It'll give you a chance to miss me..." he laughed...

"Ha ha – very funny!"

"Well we might as well get going..." Jake said as he got up...

"Okay..." Lina said as she got up...

"What time do you get off work?" Bri asked Leonard...

"Between 5 and 6..." he answered as he got up...

"Can I see you later?"

"Absolutely..." he answered as he pulled her into a kiss...

"Are you ready for me to take the check?" The waitress asked as she came back to the table...

"Yes – here you go..." Bri answered as she handed the waitress her credit card with the check...

"I'll be right back..."

"Bri – I need to go straight to work from here – can you drive?"

"Yea – why?"

"I'll go straight to work – you take the car – I'll call you when I'm ready for you to come pick me up – then we'll go to my place..."

"Okay...."

"Here you go – have a nice day..." the waitress said as she gave Bri her credit card and the receipt...

"Okay – let's go..." Jake said. When they got outside Leonard and Bri got in the car first...

"Bye!" Bri said as they pulled off in Leonard's Infinity two-seater...

"You ready?" Jake asked...

"Yes..."

"Can you drive?"

"Yes..."

"You wanna drive?"

"Hell yea!"

"Okay – let's go!" Jake exclaimed as he handed Lina they keys and they got in the car... "Oh my God – are you serious?" he laughed as Lina took a selfie of herself behind the wheel...

"You want me to delete it?"

"Just drive..." he laughed...

"Where am I going?"

"Turn on the GPS and click on Home..."

"Okay..." Jake watched Lina intently as she drove. Lina was too busy feeling herself to notice...

"We're here..."

"Wow!" Lina was in awe as soon as she stepped out of the car...

"C'mon..." he said as he took her by the hand and led her inside... "Make yourself at home..."

"You mind if I look around?"

"Not at all – just stay out of the room marked private..."

"Private? Oohhh... what's in there?"

"I work remotely from home for the Superior Court..." he lied...

"Oh okay – I won't go in there..." she said as she went upstairs. Jake smiled to himself because he knew she was going to the master bedroom... "Ooohhh... this is nice!" Jake continued smiling as he waited for her to come downstairs...

"You like what you see?"

"Yeesss..."

"C'mon – I'll show you around down here..." he said as he took her hand...

"I love how everything opens up to the backyard...

"So do I – especially in the evening..."

"I bet the sunsets are beautiful..."

"I'll show you later tonight..." he said as he pulled her into a kiss. He was relieved when Lina began to relax in his arms and he took that as a sign to go further...

"Magic... wait..."

"What's wrong?"

"I need to tell you something..." she said as she took him by the hand and led him to the couch. Jake sat down and waited for Lina to sit beside him... "I'm... I'm a virgin..."

"We don't have to do anything if you don't want to... I'm just happy you're here..."

"So you're not mad?"

"Naa..."

"Let's go outside..."

"Okay..." Jake stood up, took Lina's hand, helped her up, and led her out into the backyard...

"I wish we could get in the pool..."

"Why can't we?"

"I didn't bring a change of clothes..."

"I have clothes..."

"You have clothes for you..." she laughed...

"I can give you a pair of swim shorts and a t-shirt..."

"Okay – I'll be right back – I need to go to the bathroom..." Lina said as she hurried back inside. When she found the bathroom she ran into it, closed the door, and called Bri..

"Hey Lina..."

"I need your help..."

"Oh my God – what happened?!"

"Nothing... at least not yet..."

"Oh boy..."

35

"I don't know what to do!"

"Lina – take a deep breath..."

"I'm so nervous..."

"Everybody's nervous the first time..."

"How'd you know?"

"You're in the bathroom calling me – hello!"

"So what do I do?"

"Just relax and let him take the lead..."

"Relax and let him take the lead..."

"If you start shaking or pulling away from him – he'll stop..."

"What if he doesn't?"

"You really think he's that kinda guy?"

"No..."

"Okay then..."

"Lina?"

"Yes Magic?"

"You okay in there?"

"I'm okay – I'll be out in a minute..."

"Okay – you can change in the guest room..."

"Okay – thanks..."

"Call me later..." Bri whispered before she hung up...

"Are you okay?" Jake asked as she opened the door...

"Yea..."

"Okay – I'll see you outside..." Lina hurried to the guest room, took off her clothes, put on the swim trunks, put on the t-shirt, and went outside...

"C'mon in – the water's nice and warm..." Lina took her time getting in the water...

"How deep is this?"

"It's 3 feet, 5 feet, and 9 feet..."

"Here I am..." she said as she went up to him and put her arms around his neck...

"Here we go!" Jake exclaimed as he dunked them both under the water...

"Oh my God! My hair!"

"I thought you wanted to get in the water!" he laughed...

"Oh I wanna get in the water alright!" she said as she pushed him down...

"Oh it's like that – okay!" Lina tried to get away from him but he was too quick...

"Aaahh!" she screamed as she went down in the water. When she came back up, Jake as just standing there looking at her... "Why are you looking at me like that?" Jake didn't answer her so she looked down at herself and realized he was looking at her breasts through the wet t-shirt. She looked back at Jake and decided to take the t-shirt off...

"Wow..." he whispered as she came towards him and put her arms around his neck. Jake pulled her close and pressed her breasts up against him as he pulled her into a kiss. He was relieved when she relaxed in his arms and he started pulling her towards the 5 feet...

"What are you doing?" she whispered. Jake didn't answer her. Once he got to where the 5 feet started, he moved his hands down to her waist and began kissing and sucking on her breasts... "Ooohhh.... Magic..." she moaned. He began to kiss his way down her stomach and when he got to her belly button he slid the swim shorts off and went down under the water... "Magic... Haa..." she moaned as he spread her lips with his tongue. Lina grabbed his head with both hands as he flicked his tongue on her clit... "Magic... Ooohhh... Magic... Haa... Haa... Haa..." Jake came up out of the water, guided her towards the edge of the pool, and slid off his swim shorts. Lina wrapped her legs around his waist and her arms around his neck. Jake eased himself inside her and began making love to her... "Ooohhh Magic..."

"Lina..." Their bodies rocked together as the waves splashed against their bodies and the edge...

"Magic... I'm cumming..."

"I'm cumming with you...

"Haa... Haa... Haa..."

"Uggh! Uggh! Uggh!" Jake kissed her and began to move towards the shallow end of the pool. Lina held onto his neck and kept her legs wrapped around his waist as he carried her upstairs to the bedroom. Once he got to the bed, they fell back onto the bed and picked up where they left off...

CHAPTER 5

"Hey..." Bri said as Leonard got in...

"Hey..."

"Where to?"

"Turn on the GPS, click on Home..."

"Okay..." Leonard watched Bri intently as they drove. Bri put the window down and let her hair dance in the wind...

"Slow down – the house is on the left..."

"Ooohhh... this is nice!" Bri exclaimed as she pulled into the driveway...

"Thank you..." Bri got out the car, waited for Leonard to get out, and handed him the keys...

"I wish I had one of these..." she sighed. Leonard smiled to himself as he made a mental note of what she said...

"Welcome home..." he said as he opened the door... "C'mon – I'll show you around..." he said as he took her by the hand and pulled her inside... "I'm going to kiss you in the foyer..." he breathed as he pushed her back against the wall. Bri was surprised

when he kissed her gently and Leonard sensed it...
"Something wrong?"

"No..."

"Come with me..." he said as he grabbed her hand and pulled her towards the living room...

"This is beautiful..."

"The sunroom is over here..."

"This is beautiful too..." Leonard pulled her into the dining room and then the kitchen... "I love it..." she laughed...

"What's so funny?"

"You keep pulling me!" she laughed...

"I'm sorry – I can't help it..."

"Am I the first?"

"Yea..."

"So... how many bedrooms do you have?"

"Five..."

"Any on this floor?"

"Two..."

"Show me..."

"Come with me..." he said as he took her hand, smiled at her mischievously, and took her into the first bedroom... "This is my office..."

"This is nice..." Leonard took her out of the office and into the guest room...

"This is the guest room..."

"That bed looks comfortable..."

"You wanna test it?"

"Yea..." Bri sighed as she walked backwards towards the bed and pulled Leonard down on top of her...

"Is it comfortable?"

"I'm not done testing it..." she breathed as she pulled him into a kiss. Leonard pushed his tongue in

her mouth and began kissing her ferociously...
"Mmmph..." "Mmmmm..." "Mmmph..." "Mmmmm...
Shit!" Bri exclaimed as her phone rang...

"Don't answer it!" Leonard growled in her ear...

"Fuck!" Bri moaned as he opened her pants
and put his hand between her legs. Leonard got up
between her legs and pulled her jeans and panties
down so fast Bri was startled, but she didn't stop him
as he opened his pants, unzipped his zipper, and took
out his dick...

"Is this what you want?" he asked as he shook
his dick in his hand...

"Yeesss...." she breathed. Leonard lay down on
top of her, pushed his tongue in her mouth, and thrust
his dick inside her...

"Mmmph..."
"Mmmmm..."
"Mmmph..."
"Mmmmm..."
"Mmmph..."
"Mmmmm..."
"Mmmph..."
"Mmmmm..."
"Mmmph..."
"Mmmmm..."
"MMMPH!"
"MMMMM!"
"MMMPH!"
"MMMMM!"
"MMMPH!"
"MMMMM!"
"MMMPH!"
"MMMMM!"

"MMMPH!"
"MMMMM!"

"So..." he breathed as they continued kissing... "Is it comfortable?"

"Hell yea..."

"Are... you... sure... you... may... need... to... test... it... again..."

"I... think... I... need... to... test... the... master..."

"I... can... make... that... happen... Is that your phone?"

"Yea..."

"Answer it..." he said as he got up..."

"You sure? I thought..."

"I'm going to prep the grill – go ahead..." he answered as he put his dick back in his pants and left the room...

"What?!" Bri snapped as she answered the phone...

"I'm a slut..." Lina whispered...

"Oh shit – hold on a minute..." Bri got up, put the phone on the bed, and put the phone on speaker... "What happened?"

"Am I on speaker?"

"Yea – I'm getting dressed – go ahead...

"Damn – I'm sorry..."

"You ain't stop nothin' – talk!"

"Bri..." Lina whispered as she started crying...

"Are you okay?!"

"He was everything I ever wanted..."

"Oh thank God – you scared me..."

"I wanted to go in the pool..."

"Oooh... okay..."

"I told him I didn't have any clothes..."

"I know he has a dryer..."

"He gave me a t-shirt and some swim shorts..."

"That was nice..."

"We went in the pool... I got wet..."

"That usually happens when you go swimming..." Bri laughed...

"He was looking at me so I looked down..."

"Ooohhh..."

"My breasts were coming through the t-shirt anyway... so..."

"So what?!"

"I took the shirt off..."

"Oh my God! You are a slut!" Bri laughed...

"I wanted to be... you know..."

"A slut?" Bri laughed...

"Like you..."

"You really think I'm a slut – don't you?"

"That's not what I mean!"

"What do you mean then?"

"I wanted to be like you..."

"I don't understand..."

"You're not afraid to do what you want – you just do it..."

"Wow Lina – thanks... I guess..."

"I was scared..."

"Of him?"

"It was my first time – I didn't know what to do..."

"Ooohhh... now I get it..."

"I told him before we got in the pool..."

"That's good..."

"I thought he'd be mad..."

"Mad? Why?"

"I don't know..."

"Well the good thing is you don't have to worry about that anymore..."

"I sure don't..."

"You sound happy..."

"He did something..."

"Did he hurt you?"

"No..."

"What did he do?"

"In the water... he..."

"You had sex in the pool?"

"Yea..."

"Damn – I've always wanted to have sex in the water!"

"He went under the water... and..."

"Oh my God – he went down on you?!"

"Yea..."

"Oh shit – you lucky Bitch – I'm jealous!"

"His tongue was amazing..."

"I bet it was!"

"Did that ever happen to you?"

"Yea... it happened to me..."

"Was it amazing?"

"Hell no – I pushed him off me!" Bri laughed...

"Why would you do that?"

"He pissed me off 'cause he didn't know what the fuck he was doing!" Bri laughed...

"I bet Leonard knows what he's doing..."

"Oh hell yea..." she lied. Leonard stopped listening and went outside to prep the grill...

"Where's Len?"

"He's outside prepping the grill..."

"Oh he's cooking for you – that's nice..."

"Where's Magic?"

"He's downstairs..."

"Where are you?"

"I'm upstairs – I just woke up..."

"Le'me go see what Len's up to – I'll talk to you later..."

"Okay bye..."

"Who were you talking to?" Jake asked as he came into the bedroom...

"I was talking to Bri..." she yawed...

"How'd you sleep?"

"Like a baby..."

"C'mon downstairs – I got some steaks on the grill..."

"Okay..." Lina yawned as Jake's phone started ringing...

"Yo!"

"You just had to eat the pussy!"

"Wait... I can't..." Jake laughed...

"Your girl called Bri – and she told Bri – and I quote – his tongue was amazing!"

"Word?"

"Word!"

"Wait – how you know – Bri told you?"

"She had the phone on speaker..."

"Hey..." Lina said as she came in the backyard...

"Hey – make yourself comfortable – I'ma go inside and get the food ready..." he lied...

"Hey – how's it going out here?" Bri asked as she came into the backyard...

"I'm good – make yourself comfortable – I'm going inside to make pasta salad..." Leonard lied...

"Okay..."

"Now whatchu gonna do when she asks you where the pasta salad is?" Jake laughed...

"I can make pasta salad – that's not why I called you..."

"Damn – why you sound mad?"

"You and your girl put me on the spot..."

"How?"

"Like I said – your girl told my girl your tongue was amazing..."

"What can I say – I guess you know how I do..." he laughed...

"That's not the problem..."

"Look – it doesn't have to be a problem – just eat the pussy!" he laughed...

"It's not that..."

"What is it then?"

"Bri lied..."

"Wait – what the fuck are you talking about?"

"Your girl asked Bri if it ever happened to her..."

"Ooohhh... I get it..."

"No you don't..."

"Wait – Len – what's going on?"

"Bri told your girl the last time somebody went down on her she pushed him off her 'cause he pissed her off..."

"Oh shit – she didn't like it?"

"She said he didn't know what the fuck he was doing!"

"Oh damn!"

"So your girl said I bet Len knows what he's doing and Bri lied..."

"Oh damn – she didn't like it with you either?!"

"I didn't go down on her..."

"What?! Why?!"

"See – I shouldn't a said anything..."

"I'm glad you did..."

"Why – so you can clown me?"

"I'm not trying to clown you – I'm trying to help you!"

"Really? You try'na help me eat pussy?"

"Look – we both know that's why you called me – so let me help you..."

"I can't believe I'm having this conversation..."

"Okay – class is in session – take notes..."

"Hold on – le'me get..."

"Oh my God! I mean pay attention!" Jake laughed...

"Well say that then!"

"Okay – you're going to start by treating the pussy like you treat her mouth..."

"How am I supposed to do that with all that hair down there?"

"Women kiss men with beards and mustaches all day every day – if they can do it – you can do it!"

"Okay – I'm listening..."

"The first thing you're gonna do is kiss her pubic area..."

"Where the hair is?"

"That's the pubic area right?"

"Why am I kissing her pubic area?"

"Because it'll turn her on..."

"Ooohhh – okay..."

"You're gonna kiss her outer lips, then you're gonna spread her outer lips with your fingers so you can see her clit..."

"And then I suck it?"

"No – you're gonna get real close to it and breathe on it..."

"Why am I gonna breathe on it?" Leonard laughed...

"Cause when she feels your breath on her clit – it'll drive her crazy..."

"Ooohhh..."

"When she starts squirming around, you start flicking her clit with your tongue..."

"Okay..."

"She's gonna start moaning if you're making her feel good and that's when you hold onto her thighs and dive in..."

"Dive in?"

"Dive in – slide your tongue all over, all around, dip the tongue in, pull it out, suck on her clit, repeat..."

"Oh damn! You make me wanna go outside and do her right now!"

"Not yet..."

"Not yet?"

"You need to take cues from her – listen to her moans – if she grabs the sides of your head and starts riding your face – you have her right where you want her..."

"I like the sound of that..."

"You'll love it – and in that moment you can break her..."

Tracy Wilson

"I don't wanna hurt her!"

"That's not what I mean – I mean once she grabs your head and starts riding your face – she's cumming..."

"Ooohhh!!"

"And if her legs start trembling – hold on – 'cause it's gonna be intense!"

"Oh shit!"

"Now listen – this is important..."

"Okay – I'm listening!"

"After she cums – she's gonna want you to stop – she'll tell you it's sensitive – but you don't stop..."

"What?"

"You don't stop – you do it a little slower... and a lot softer..."

"Why don't I just stop?"

"Cause she's going to have mini-gasms..."

"Mini-gasms?"

"Yea – she'll have an intense orgasm – and then she'll have a couple of small orgasms because her clit is still sensitive..."

"Oh damn!"

"I bet Bri can suck a mean dick..."

"She probably can..."

"Le'me ask you – how'd you do all that in the pool?"

"I didn't..."

"I didn't think so – you would've drowned..."

"I did enough though..."

"I need you to have a pool party!" Leonard laughed...

"I need you to pay attention to what I'm about to tell you..."

"Okay – I'm listening!"

"After you finish – you come up between her legs, you push her legs back so her feet are on her shoulders – you put your dick inside her, and you kiss her – and when you kiss her – put your tongue in her mouth while you're fucking her..."

"Wait a minute – she won't think that's nasty?!"

"Trust me..."

"So wait – you did all that with Lina?"

"Not yet – she was a virgin – I gotta make love to her a few times before I fuck her..."

"Le'me call you later..." Leonard said as he hung up abruptly...

"You still on the phone?" Bri asked...

"I was..."

"Is the pasta salad ready?"

"Yea..."

"You need any help?"

"Sure – you can bring out the ice tea – the pitcher is in the fridge..."

"Hey..." Lina said as she came into the kitchen...

"Hey..." Jake breathed as he pulled her into a kiss...

"You need any help?"

"Sure – I got potato salad and sangria in the fridge..."

"I'll get the sangria..." she said as she went to open the fridge...

CHAPTER 6

"Those steaks look good!" Bri exclaimed...

"They taste better than they look..." Leonard said as he cut a small piece, put it on a fork, and held it up to her mouth...

"Oh my God..." she sighed as she chewed...

"Told you..."

"It's so tender... so juicy..."

"I know..."

"How do you do that?"

"For starters, I use propane..."

"You don't use charcoal?"

"Nope..."

"Why?"

"I don't like the taste of it..."

"Really? I'm surprised..."

"People use charcoal and lighter fluid without a second thought – but you have to be careful – the charcoal you're burning goes into the meat and into your lungs..."

"I never thought of that..."

"Don't get me wrong – I've been to a lot of barbeques where they use charcoal, they have a pig roasting over a fire, etc. – I just prefer the taste of meat cooked over propane..."

"Well now that I've tasted it – I'm sold..."

"With propane, you can lower the flame, close the grill, and let the food cook from the inside – it cooks better, it tastes better, and you get a tender, juicy steak instead of a tough, dry one..." Bri bust out laughing...

"What's so funny?"

"Hank Hill..." she laughed...

"Huh?"

"The cartoon – King of The Hill..."

"Yep..." Leonard said as he mimicked Hank and they both laughed...

"Ready to eat?" Jake asked...

"I sure am..."

"Le'me hurry up and feed you then... you need stamina..."

"I need stamina?"

"You haven't eaten anything since breakfast – I can't have you passing out on me..."

"I can't believe I fell asleep..." Lina said as she poured two glasses of Sangria...

"I'm not surprised – you didn't really sleep last night..."

"That's true..."

"Here you go..." he said as he put a plate in front of her... "Taste it – tell me what you think..." Lina tasted the potato salad first...

"Oh my God! This is so good!"

"Try the steak..."

"Mmmm!"

"I'm glad you like it..." he said as they started eating...

"I'm glad you can cook..."

"Does that mean you can't cook?"

"I can cook... when I have to..."

"When you have to? Don't you eat?"

"I eat – but I don't cook a lot..."

"Why not?"

"I don't like leftovers that much..."

"Are you saying we have to eat all this tonight?"

"This is different..."

"What's the difference?"

"I didn't cook it..." she laughed...

"So let's say you cook for me ‐ and let's say we have leftovers – what do you do with them?"

"That depends on what I cook..."

"You really don't like leftovers!" Jake laughed as they continued eating...

"So how's the pasta salad?" Leonard asked...

"Delicious – I'm glad you made it..."

"You like pasta salad?" he asked as he poured them both some ice tea...

"I love it – but I don't get it often..."

"Why not?"

"Most of the cook outs I go to have potato salad..."

"You don't like potato salad?'

"I do – but I prefer pasta salad..."

"I'm glad I made it for you..."

"How'd you know I like pasta salad?"

"I have a confession to make..."

"Okay..."

"I was planning to make potato salad – but I ran out of potatoes..." he laughed...

"God works in mysterious ways!" Bri exclaimed as they both laughed and continued eating...

"So... how do you feel?" Jake asked...

"I feel better now that I've had something to eat..." Lina answered...

"How do you feel about what happened earlier?"

"I'm not sure..."

"What do you mean by that?"

"It's hard to explain..."

"Just say what you feel..."

"Well... I thought I would feel... different..."

"Different?"

"I don't know why this is so hard..." she sighed...

"You thought you'd feel like a woman?"

"Yea..."

"You don't have to worry about that..."

"I don't?"

"Lina – you are definitely a woman – a beautiful, passionate, and sexy, woman..."

"You think I'm beautiful, passionate, and sexy?"

"Oh yea..."

"Well... I think you're sexy too..."

"Oh yea? What else do you think about me?"

"Ummm... your tongue... is amazing..." Jake smiled. He could tell the sangria was having a calming, relaxing effect on Lina and he was ready to take advantage of it...

"So..." he said as he moved closer to her and pulled her close enough to whisper in her ear... "Would you like to feel my tongue again?" he whispered as he wrapped his arm around her. Lina didn't answer him so he began kissing her on her neck...

"Yeesss..."

"Yes what?" he breathed as he kissed her...

"I... want... to... feel... your... tongue... again..."

"Come with me..." Leonard said as he stood up and extended his hand. Bri took his hand and Leonard led her into the kitchen, through the living room, and up the stairs...

"This is nice!" she exclaimed...

"I'm glad you like it..." he said as he led her out the first room and into the second room...

"This is nice too..."

"I'm glad you like it..." he said as he led her down the hall towards the master...

"You get a lot of sunlight up here..."

"Wait until you see the sunset..." he said as he led her into the master bedroom...

"Oh Len... this is beautiful!" Leonard didn't say anything. He just smiled as she went around the room, went into the master bath, and came back into the room where he was...

"Come with me..." he said as he took her by the hand and led her onto the private deck...

"Oh Len!" she sighed...

"I love to sit out here sometimes, enjoy the peace, and watch the sun go down..."

"I could definitely see myself sitting out here having coffee in the morning..."

"I'm glad you're spending the night..." he breathed as he pulled her into a kiss...

"Don't move..." Jake commanded. Lina was immediately turned on by his tone. She did as she was told. Jake pulled her close to him so fast it startled her...

"Ooohh!" He began kissing her softly at first and then he began to kiss her harder. Lina kissed him back just as hard as he lifted up her arms. They continued kissing as he pulled her shirt up. He stopped kissing her long enough to pull the shirt over her head and he began kissing her again as he moved his hands down her back to unfasten her bra. He stopped kissing her to remove her bra and then he stood back to look at her. Lina continued to stand still as she was told. He went back towards her, pulled her close to him, and began kissing her on her neck as she began to pull his shirt up...

"I told you don't move..." he breathed in her ear...

"I'm not listening..." she giggled as she pulled his shirt up over his head and threw it across the room...

"Get on the bed..." he commanded as he pushed her back towards the bed. Lina was startled when she fell back on it...

"Oooh!" Jake got on the bed on his knees, went in between her legs, and snatched her jeans and panties off in one quick motion. Lina was startled but Jake got on top of her before she had a chance to react...

"Tell me what you want..." he growled in her ear...

"I... I want..."

"Say it!!" he commanded...

"Your tongue!!" Jake knew exactly what he was doing and Lina was responding just as he thought she would...

"Mmm..." he moaned as he took her left breast in his mouth...

"Magic..." she moaned. He moved over to the right breast and took it in his mouth as he continued to play with the left one...

"Oh Magic..." she moaned. Jake was ready to give her everything he couldn't give her in the pool and he began kissing her down her stomach...

"Come here..." Leonard said as he led Bri over to the chaise lounge and sat her down. He sat down beside her and began lifting up her shirt...

"Len..."

"Ssshhh..." he whispered as he pulled her shirt over her head. Bri sat still as Leonard looked at her. He pulled her closer, unclasped her bra, and slid it off. Bri sat quiet, looking back at him, wondering what he was going to do next...

"Lay back..." he said as he pushed her down gently. He smiled at her and admired her breasts as the sunlight went across her nipples...

"You like what you see?"

"Ssshhh..." he whispered as he took off his shirt. Bri was turned on when she saw him in the sunlight. She wasn't prepared for what happened next...

"Oh my God..." she breathed as he dropped his pants...

"I take it you like what you see?" he asked as he moved towards her, fully erect...

"Yeeessss..." she breathed as she reached out to grab his dick...

"Uh uh..." he said as he stepped back...

"But I..."

"Ssshhh..." he interrupted as he got on the chaise lounge on his knees, went in between her legs, and snatched off her jeans and panties...

"Oh Len..." she breathed...

"MAGIC!!" Lina moaned as Jake flicked his tongue on her clit. This was the moment he was waiting for and he wasn't about to disappoint her... "Magic... Magic... Magic..." Lina was moaning continuously and it was music to Jake's ears as he grabbed her thighs and dove in...

"Len... shit..." Bri moaned as he started flicking his tongue on her clit. He wanted to take her clit in his mouth and suck the shit out of it, but he remembered what Jake told him and decided to grab her thighs and dive in instead...

"Magic... Don't stop..." Lina moaned as she grabbed Jake's head with her hands and began riding his face. When her legs began trembling, he applied more pressure with his tongue... "MAGIC!! I'M CUMMING!!" she screamed as she smothered his face. Fortunately, Jake had plenty of experience in holding his breath...

"LEN... FUCK... LEN!!" Bri moaned as she grabbed Leonard's head and began riding his face. Leonard was startled when she locked her legs around his head but when they started trembling; he knew what time it was... "I'M CUMMING!! AAAGGGHHH!!" Leonard remembered what Jake told him and instead of stopping, he stuck his tongue inside her...

"Magic..." Lina whispered as he continued licking, slurping, and sucking softly. Lina didn't bother to try and push him away as her legs were still trembling from mini-gasms. He stopped and when he saw the dazed look in her eyes, he knew it was time...

"Oh shit... Len... Ooohhh..." Leonard licked around her Bri's clit, stuck his tongue back in, and then licked around her clit again. Just when he was about to stop, Bri surprised him by grabbing his head with her hands and ridding his face again...

Jake stood up, removed his pants, and stood in front of Lina so she could see him fully erect...
"Oohhh..." Lina whispered. He got back on the bed on his knees, pushed her legs up, and eased himself inside her... "Magic..." she moaned. Jake pushed her legs down, spread them so her feet were touching her shoulders, laid down on her, and pushed is tongue in her mouth as he began making love to her...

"LEN... DON'T STOP... I'M CUMMING AGAIN... AAAGGGHHH!!" This was exactly where Leonard wanted Bri and this time he didn't take

Jake's advice - he pushed Bri's legs down, got up between her legs, thrust himself inside her, and pushed his tongue in her mouth as he fucked her...

"MMMPH!! MMMPH!! MMMPH!!"

"MMMM!! MMMM!! MMMM!!" Jake was in trouble. Up until now, he was able to control his urge to fuck the shit out of Lina, but he was about to lose it. What he didn't know was Lina was also losing control just as much as he was − and when she grabbed his ass with her hands and pushed him in deeper, that was all he needed...

"MMMPH!! MMMPH!! MMMPH!!"

"MMMM!! MMMM!! MMMM!!"

"MMMPH!! MMMPH!! MMMPH!!"

"MMMM!! MMMM!! MMMM!!" Leonard was on a mission to seek Bri's G Spot and by her moans he knew he'd found it... "MMMPH!! MMMPH!! MMMPH!!"

"MMMM!! MMMM!! MMMM!!"

Jake collapsed on top of Lina and moved her legs down as he kissed her. Lina wrapped her legs around him and locked her feet together as they continued kissing...

"Damn..." Leonard breathed as he kissed Bri...

"I think everybody in the neighborhood knows your name now..." she laughed...

"I know a few of my neighbor's names too..."

"Oh shit..." she laughed...

CHAPTER 7

"I'ma go downstairs and put the food away..." Jake said as he got up...

"I'll help you..." Lina said...

"Stay there... I got it..."

"Okay..." she sighed... "What's wrong?"

"Nothing..." he sighed...

"Nothing?"

"You're glowing..."

"Bri..."

"Huh?"

"Wake up..."

"Why?"

"The sun's going down..."

"Okay..."

"Bri..."

"Huh?"

"Look..." Bri sat up and opened her eyes...

"Oh Len... It's beautiful..."

"I wanted you to see it..."

"I'm glad you woke me up..."

"I'm going to put the food away – be in bed when I get back..."

"Yes Daddy..."

"Yo!" Jake answered...

"Mission accomplished!" Leonard exclaimed...

"You're welcome..."

"I'm glad I listened in on their conversation..."

"Be careful with that..."

"Why? Everything worked out..."

"You got lucky..."

"Damn right I got lucky..."

"So how was it?"

"It was better than I imagined..."

"Same here..."

"Really?"

"Yea..."

"So are you gonna marry this one?"

"I might..."

"You might?"

"I need to make sure I can trust her with my heart..."

"Bri already has mine..."

"I know..."

"How you know?"

"You asked me for my help – you wouldn't have asked me for help if you didn't care about her..."

"I still can't believe we had that conversation..." Leonard laughed...

"Well it's not like you can ask your father!" Jake laughed...

"I'd never ask my father!" Leonard laughed...

"Thank God I never had to ask mine!" Jake laughed...

"I wonder if my Dad ate pussy..."

"If he's anything like my father – he ate pussy!" Jake laughed...

"How do you know? It's not like you were in the room with them!" Leonard laughed...

"Yes I was..."

"Wait... Wait... Wait..."

"One night when I was little, I walked in on them..."

"You saw your father eat your mother's pussy?!"

"I saw them naked and I saw his head between her legs – I thought my mother was having another baby and he was helping the baby come out!" Jake laughed...

"Oh my God – that's so cute!" Leonard laughed...

"I asked my mother when the baby was coming!" Jake laughed...

"That's so cute!" Leonard laughed...

"You should've seen the look on my father's face when I told him I saw him trying to help Mommy push the baby out!" Jake laughed...

"Oh my God... stop... my stomach!" Leonard laughed...

"My mother told me my father was checking to make sure the baby was okay! Aaaa haaaa haaaa haaa!"

"Did your mother ever get pregnant after she had you?"

"Naa..."

"So how did they explain the baby?"

"I overheard my parents talking about sex one day – once I heard that – I stopped asking – I didn't think any more about it until I started watching porn..."

"Your father would be so proud..." Leonard laughed...

"Shut the fuck up!" Jake laughed...

"What are we gonna tell our sons?"

"I'll have the talk with my son – but I'm not telling my son how to eat pussy!" Jake laughed...

"I wonder if mothers talk to their daughters about suckin' dick..."

"Absolutely!"

"Are you serious?"

"I sure am – they tell them it's nasty, only whores do it, they're going to hell, it's a sin, and they'll catch a disease..."

"Okay stop – you're ruining my fantasy..." Leonard laughed...

"I don't really care about that..."

"Are you serious?!"

"I'm serious..."

"Why?"

"I don't want a woman to suck my dick because she thinks that's what I want..."

"What if she wants to suck your dick because she likes sucking dick?"

"That's different – but if she doesn't want to – that's fine..."

"I think Bri wanted to suck my dick..."

"What makes you say that?"

"Earlier tonight – she tried to grab it..."

"You sure she just didn't want you to fuck her?"

"She was lying down – and I was standing in front of her..."

"Maybe you're right..."

"I hope so – I know one thing – if she wants to suck my dick – I'm all in!" he laughed...

"Le'me go – I have a beautiful woman waiting in my bed..."

"I know that's right!" Leonard laughed as they both hung up...

"Lina?" Jake called out when he saw she wasn't in the bed... "Lina – where are you?" he called out again as he went to look in the bathroom. When he got there, he stood and listened to her sing, 'I Wanna Be Down,' by Brandi...

"I wanna be down with what you're going through, I wanna be down, I wanna be down with you..." she sang. Jake took his phone out of his pocket, put it on video, and hit record as she started swaying her body and continued singing...

"I would like to get to know if I could be the kind of girl that you could be down for, 'cause when I look at you I feel something tell me that you're the kind of guy that I should make a move on, and if I don't let you know then it won't be for real, I could be wrong but I feel like something could be going on, the more I see you I the more that it becomes so true, there ain't no other for me it's only you..."

"Is that right?" Jake asked...

"Aaah! How long have you been standing there?"

"Long enough to know you have a beautiful voice..."

"Thank you..."

"May I join you?"

"Okay..." she sighed. Jake stepped into the shower and pulled her close to him...

"Sing to me..." he commanded. Bri started singing 'I Wanna Be Down,' by Brandi again...

"I wanna be down with what you're going through, I wanna be down, I wanna be down with you, no matter the time of day or night it's true I wanna be down..."

"Well shit!" Leonard laughed as he came into the bedroom. Bri was sleeping soundly... "Here we go again..." He sighed as he got in bed with her, spooned her, and went to sleep...

CHAPTER 8

Jake watched the video he recorded as Lina slept. The sun was coming in the window and there were streaks across her nipples. He loved how peaceful she looked. He tried not to wake her but when he went across her nipple, she opened her eyes...

"Good morning..." she yawned...

"Good morning..."

"How long have you been awake?"

"Not long..."

"I need coffee..."

"I can make you some coffee..." he breathed as he kissed her...

"I'll make it..." she said as she threw back the sheets and got up...

"Umm... Lina?"

"Yes Magic?"

"I have a situation that needs to be addressed..." he said as he pulled back the sheets...

"Oh my – it looks like you have an emergency..."

"Do you think I need to go to the hospital?"

"Le'me take your temperature..." she said as she got back in bed...

"Good morning..." Leonard said...

"Good morning..." Bri yawned...

"You fell asleep on me again..."

"I know... I couldn't help it – this bed is so comfortable..." she said as she stretched...

"I'm glad you slept..."

"Why didn't you wake me?"

"You looked so peaceful..."

"I can make it up to you..." she said as she got on top of him...

"Oh yea?"

"Yea..." she breathed as she began kissing him down his stomach...

"So..." Jake breathed... "Do you think I'll be okay?"

"You'll be okay..." Lina breathed... "But I'll need to see you for a follow up – in case you need more treatments..."

"I like the sound of that..."

"I like the feel of it..." she said as she pulled him into a kiss...

"I'll go make you some coffee..."

"I'll make it!" she exclaimed as she jumped up out the bed, grabbed his robe, and hurried downstairs...

"Damn!" Leonard breathed...

"You're welcome..." Bri breathed...

"You wanted to do that yesterday..."

"Yea..."

"I knew it..."

"I was wondering why you stopped me..."

"Are you still wondering?"

"Oh no..."

"Good... "

"You need coffee?"

"I'll go make some..." he said as he got out of bed...

"I'll be down in a minute..."

"Oh no you don't – you're coming downstairs with me..." he laughed...

"Why can't I stay up here?" she laughed...

"Because you have a habit of falling asleep on me..." he laughed...

"Tell you what..." she said as she got up, walked over to him, and put her arms around his neck... "If I fall asleep..." she breathed as she kissed him... "You wake me up..." she breathed as she kissed him again... "And I'll make it up to you again..."

"Okay!" he exclaimed as he hurried downstairs. Bri took his robe from behind the door, put it on, and went to sit outside on the deck...

"Have you seen my phone?" Lina asked as Jake came into the kitchen...

"It's right here..." he answered as he picked her phone up off the counter and handed it to her...

"Thanks..."

"Who are you calling?"

"I'm not calling anyone – I'm ordering from Uber Eats..."

"I have food!" he laughed...

"Trust me..." she said as she handed him a cup of coffee...

"Coffee with French vanilla creamer, scrambled eggs, sausage, potatoes, and French toast – I got this!" Leonard exclaimed as he took out the frying pans and went to the refrigerator...

"You make good coffee..." Jake said...

"Thank you..." Lina said as she went into the living room...

"Where are you going?"

"The delivery is here..." Lina answered as she opened the door...

"Bri?" Leonard called out...

"I'm out here..." she answered. Leonard went outside on the deck...

"Here's your coffee..."

"Thank you..."

"I'll be back..."

"Where are you going?"

"To make breakfast..." he answered as he went back downstairs...

"So what are we having for breakfast?" Jake asked...

"Moroccan Breakfast Skillet..."

"Where'd you order that from?"

"I didn't order it – I'm going to cook it..." she answered as she started taking everything out the bag...

Tracy Wilson

"Well shit!" Leonard laughed as he brought the tray out on the deck. He sat the tray down on the table, went over to Bri, and touched her on the cheek... "Bri..."

"Huh?"

"Breakfast is ready..."

"Oh shoot – I fell asleep again – I'm sorry – I..."

"Ssshhh..." he whispered as he kissed her...

Jake watched Lina intently as she began cooking. She removed the stems from the Swiss Chard (leafy green vegetable), chopped them up, and put them in a bowl. She did the same to the leaves and put them in a separate bowl.

Lina took the black frying pan out the cabinet and put it on the stove. She put the ground turkey and sausage in the frying pan, broke it up with a spoon, turned on the heat, and cooked it. After 5 minutes, she turned off the heat, transferred the cooked meat to a large bowl, and left the fat in the pan.

Lina took the sweet potato, cleaned it, chopped it into cubes, cooked it for 5 minutes, added the chard stems, and continued cooking them for 3 minutes. She added garlic, turmeric, sea salt, cinnamon, continued cooking the mixture until the sweet potato was tender, and added the chard leaves. She let the mixture cook for another 2 minutes, turned off the heat, mixed in the ground turkey and sausage, and made two plates.

Jake thought she was done until she went in the refrigerator and got four eggs. She carefully opened the eggs to keep from breaking the yolk and cooked them sunny-side up. When she was done, she put two eggs on top of each plate...

"Let's go eat outside..." she said...

"Okay..." he sighed... "Lord, please don't let this be nasty..." he prayed under his breath...

"I hope you like it..." she said as they sat down...

"I'm sure I will..." he lied. He wasn't sure about anything – he was actually afraid he'd want to spit it out... "Oh shit!" he exclaimed... "What's this called again?"

"Moroccan Breakfast Skillet..."

"I like it..."

"Really? You're not just saying that?"

"I really like it..."

"Oh thank God!"

"Amen!"

"You didn't think you'd like it – did you?" she laughed...

"Well... No..." he laughed...

"I wanted to make you something special..."

"You could've made me eggs, bacon, and toast and that would've been special..."

"What's so special about that?"

"It's not the food that would've made it special – it's the fact that you cooked it for me that would've made it special..."

"Aww... that's sweet..."

"So tell me – what's special about the Moroccan Breakfast Skillet?"

"I'm Moroccan..."

"Is that Dominican?"

"No – Morocco is a country in Northern Africa..."

"Oh wow..."

"My last name is Bourequat..."

"Bourequat..."

"My father's name is Youssef and my mother's name is Lina..."

"So you were named after your mother..."

"Yes..."

"What language do they speak in Morocco?"

"Arabic..."

"Can you speak Arabic?"

"Yes – that's how I got the job with the law firm..."

"Is your name Arabic?"

"Yes – my name is Arabic but also has roots in France and China. In Arabic my name means tenderness and delicate – in Chinese my name means pretty – and in France my name means elegant..."

"I can see that..." Jake said as he smiled... "Do your parents live here?"

"No – they stayed in Morocco..."

"Do you visit them often?"

"Not as often as I'd like..."

"Why? Is it too far?"

"It's not that – it's an 18-hour flight from Los Angeles to Casablanca, I have 2 lay-overs, and it's over $1,000 round-trip..."

"I'd like to meet your parents..."

"Is your last name Johnson like the NBA player?"

"No – my last name is Thompson..."

"Ooohhh..."

"So what would you like to do for the rest of the day?"

"I'd love to stay here... but I need to go home..."

"Don't worry – you'll be back soon..."

"I know..." she laughed...

"Did you enjoy your breakfast?" Leonard asked...

"Yes..." Bri answered...

"I can't believe you fell asleep again..." he laughed...

"Especially after I drank my coffee..."

"Can I ask you something?"

"Sure..."

"Is your name really Bri?"

"Yes – why?"

"So it's not short for Sabrina?"

"Oh no – thank God – I don't like that name..."

"Okay!" he laughed...

"My name is spelled B-R-I not B-R-E-E..."

"What's your last name?"

"Cooper..."

"Pleased to meet you Miss Cooper – I'm Mr. Allen..."

"Hmmm... Bri Allen... yea... I like that..."

"What would you like to do for the rest of the day?"

"I'd love to stay here – but I need to go home – I start at 7 a.m. tomorrow..."

"Okay – I'll take you home – under one condition..."

"What's that?"

"You promised you'd make it up to me if you fell asleep again..."

"Yes..."

"So how 'bout we go back to bed and make it up to each other?"

"I like the sound of that..."

CHAPTER 9

"Eeek! Eeek! Eeek! Eeek! Eeek!"

"Oh my God – shut up!" Bri yelled as she banged on her alarm clock... "Coffee on deck..." she yawned as she got out the bed, put on her robe, and went into the kitchen... "Ooohhh yeesss..." she breathed as she inhaled the aroma. She went to the cabinet, took down her favorite mug, and poured herself a cup... "I wish Len was here..." she sighed...

"Who's Len?" the man asked...

"OH MY GOD – SOMEBODY HELP ME!" she screamed as the mug hit the floor...

"Eeek! Eeek! Eeek! Eeek! Eeek!"

"Alright, alright – I'm up!" Leonard exclaimed as he jumped up out of bed... "Today is going to be a great day..." he sighed as he went towards the bathroom... "Time for a little music..." he said as he turned on the radio and jazz came through the speaker. Leonard stepped into the shower, washed himself, and stepped out... "And now for a quick

76

shave before I get dressed and go surprise my lady..."
he said as he prepped his face...

"Clean that up..." the man said as he sat down
at the table...
"GET   THE   FUCK   OUTTA   MY
APARTMENT!!" Bri screamed...
"I'm not going to tell you again..." he said as he
pointed the gun at her. Bri went to get the broom out
of the closet... "Don't try anything stupid – I don't
want to have to hurt you..."
"I need you to leave – I'm going to be late for
work..."
"I know you have time for a quickie – you don't
leave the apartment for another 30 minutes..."

"Im on my way Bri!" Leonard exclaimed as he
got in the car..."

"How do you know?"
"I've been watching you for a while..." the man
interrupted...
"Watching me?"
"I know what days you go in at 7 a.m.... I know
what days you go in at 12..."
"How long have you been watching me..." she
asked as she finished cleaning up the broken mug...
"Let's go..." he said as he stood up...
"No..."
"Do I need to remind you of what's at stake?"
he asked as he pointed the gun at her...
"I'm very aware of what's at stake!!" Bri gritted
as she grabbed the coffeepot off the coffee maker and
aimed at his head...

"AAAAGGGHHH!!" he yelled as blood poured from his head... "You're going to regret that!!" he gritted...

"And you're going to regret coming in here!!" Leonard growled as he lunged for the man, knocked him to the floor, and the gun went off...

"LEEENNN!!" Bri screamed...

"POLICE!! DON'T YOU MOVE!!" the officer yelled as he put the gun to the back of Leonard's head...

"IT WASN'T HIM!!" Bri screamed. The officer stepped back as another one came in...

"What's going on?" the officer asked as Leonard got up...

"He broke into my apartment!!" Bri exclaimed, pointing at the man on the floor...

"Is that his gun?"

"YES!!" Bri and Leonard exclaimed...

"What the... ooohhh... my head... officers... thank God you're here... these people..."

"You're under arrest..." the second officer said as he helped the man up off the floor and cuffed him...

"I'm under arrest?! I'm the victim!!"

"Oh my God – are you okay?!" Bri's neighbor asked as she came into the kitchen...

"Who are you?" the first detective asked...

"I'm the one who called you..." she answered...

"Ms. Carter? You called the police?" Bri asked...

"Yes – I've seen him lurking around – I knew he was up to no good when he came in the building this morning!!"

"Well 'Victim,' as I was saying... you're under arrest for breaking and entering and attempted robbery..." the second officer said...

"And attempted rape!!" Bri exclaimed...

"I NEVER RAPED YOU!!" the man yelled...

"Officer – when I came in I heard him tell my lady he knew she had time for a quickie because he's been watching her!!" Leonard exclaimed...

"You have the right to remain silent... anything you say can and will be used against you in a court of law... you have the right to an attorney..." the second officer continued as Lina walked in...

"Bri – are you okay?!"

"Lina!!" Bri cried as she ran to Lina and broke down...

"What happened?!"

"He broke in here... he..."

"Lina Bourequat?" the first officer asked...

"Yes?"

"I'm glad you're here..."

"You are?" Lina and Bri both asked in unison...

"Okay – we need everyone to come down to the station so we can get your statements – Ms. Bourequat – we'll speak with you after we finish with them..."

"Bri – you're coming with me!!" Leonard exclaimed...

"I'll go get dressed..."

"Ms. Bourequat – you can ride with us..." the first officer said...

"No thank you..." Lina said as she called Jake...

"Good morning beautiful..." he answered...

"Can you come get me?"

"What's wrong?"

"I'm with Bri... Len's here... someone broke in her apartment... the police..."

"I'll be right there!!" Jake exclaimed as he hurried to his car...

"If you cannot afford an attorney one will be provided for you - do you understand the rights I have just read to you?" the second officer asked the man as he opened the door to the squad car...

"FUCK YOU!!" the man yelled...

"I take it that means you understand!!" the officer gritted as he pushed him in the car head first...

CHAPTER 10

"Lina..." Jake breathed as he ran towards her...

"Magic..." she whispered as he held her in his arms... "I gotchu..." he said as she started shaking... "What happened?"

"Can you take me downtown to the police station?"

"Of course – but you're shaking – I know whatever happened – it's bad..."

"Can we get some coffee?"

"Sure – c'mon..." he said as he walked her to the car and opened the door for her. After he got in, he took Lina's hand... "I'm here for you – but I need to know what's going on..."

"Can I have some coffee first? Please?"

"Okay..." Jake drove to the Pantry Café and parked...

"I'll be right back..."

"Okay..." Lina watched him go inside the restaurant before she took out her phone...

"You've reached the office of Jennifer Schemerhorn at Adams & Martin. My office hours are 9 a.m. to 5 p.m. If you are calling after hours, please leave a detailed message. If this is an emergency, please press zero to be connected with someone who can assist you..."

"Hi Jennifer - it's Lina. I know we have to prepare the contract today for the new hire, but I have an emergency. I'll call you back later today and let you know if I can make it in..."

"Here's your coffee..." Jake said as he got in the car and handed it to Lina...

"Thank you..."

"We had a deal – you got your coffee so..."

"I saw the police outside so I went to check on Bri..."

"Bri?! What happened with Bri?!"

"Somebody broke into her apartment..."

"Is she alright?!"

"Yea – thank God – her neighbor called the police and Len was there..."

"What the fuck is going on?!" Jake exclaimed as he hit the steering wheel...

"He wanted... to... rape her..."

"WHAT?!"

"Len said he heard the man tell her he knew she had time for a quickie..."

"THE FUCK?!"

"I'm scared..."

"Why?! Didn't they get him?!"

"They did... but..." Jake pulled the car over...

"Lina..." he said as he took her hand...

"The officer knew my name..."

"Okay – maybe he heard Bri call your name..."

"He called me by my full name – he said he was glad I was there..."

"That doesn't make any sense..."

"He said they needed to speak to me – he wanted me to get in the car with them – I told him no thank you..."

"I don't blame you..."

"Will you stay with me?"

"I'm staying with you – let's go!!" he exclaimed as they headed downtown...

"We got him Lieutenant!" Captain Oddo said as he brought the man inside the precinct...

"Who we got?" Lieutenant Fox asked...

"The rapist! We got him!"

"Hot damn!" Lieutenant Fox exclaimed as Bri, Leonard, and Ms. Carter came in with Captain Tippet...

"Ms. Cooper, Ms. Carter, and... Who are you sir?"

"I'm Leonard Allen..."

"Come with me..." Captain Tippet said as he motioned for them to follow him down the hall...

"I'm bleeding!!" the man yelled...

"Sit your ass down!!" Captain Oddo snapped as he pushed the man down in the chair and cuffed him to the desk... "Here's how this is going to go – you're going to write a confession – you're going to sign it – I'm going to witness it – and you're going to go from here to the infirmary – from the infirmary you're going to go to a cell – and after you get in your cell – make sure you accept Jesus as your Savior so you don't rot in hell when they kill your ass!!"

"I'll take my chances at trial!!" the man laughed...

"What makes you think you're going to make it to trial?" Captain Oddo asked. The expression on the man's face changed from amused to terror...

"You can't do that to me!! I have rights!!" Captain Oddo smiled a sinister smile before he left the man in the room and went into the room with Captain Tippet...

"I'm Captain Jonathan Tippet and this is Captain Anthony Oddo – we're going to take a statement from each of you – separately..."

"Separately?" Bri asked...

"Yes – we need to get your statements without the other people in the room..."

"Why can't I stay with her?" Leonard asked...

"Because we want the charges to stick –Ms. Carter – I'm going to start with you – Ms. Cooper – you're going to go in another room with Captain Oddo – Mr. Allen – please go wait in the hallway..."

"The hallway?"

"Yes – after I get Ms. Carter's statement I'm going to take your statement..."

"What about Bri?"

"Captain Oddo is taking her statement..."

"Fine..." Leonard sighed as he left the room...

"Ms. Carter – may I have your full name?"

"My name is Lorraine..." she said as she touched his hand...

"Ms. Carter – I'm flattered – but I'm happily married..."

"Can't blame a lady for trying..."

"Why'd you call us this morning?"

"Every morning I get up at 5 a.m. – I make myself a cup of coffee, I light a cigarette, I sit in the living room by my window, and I look out the window..."

"Does your window face the street?"

"Yes..."

"How many times have you seen the man before today?"

"He's been standing in front of our building for the last two weeks..."

"He just stands outside?"

"He stands outside until he sees Bri – Ms. Cooper – after she comes out the building – he leaves..."

"What happened today?"

"I was sitting in my window, smoking my cigarette, and drinking my coffee. I saw him come to the building – somebody left out – and he went in..."

"He got in the building because someone came out?"

"Yes – and I called as soon as I saw him!!"

"You did a good thing Ms. Carter..."

"I knew he was up to no good!!"

"Okay – here's your statement – read it over and if everything looks good – print your name, sign your name, and date it..."

"Ms. Cooper – please tell me what happened..." Captain Oddo said as he began writing...

"My first name is spelled B-R-I..."

"Thank you – go ahead..."

"I set my alarm for 5:30 a.m. The alarm went off and I got out of my bed. I put my robe on and went into the kitchen to make myself a cup of coffee..."

"Did you see the man that broke into your apartment when you went into your kitchen?"

"No..."

"Okay – go ahead..."

"I made myself a cup of coffee, I sat down at the table, and I said out loud I wish Len was here..."

"Who's Len?"

"Leonard Allen – he's the man who's head you put your gun too..."

"I'm sorry about that..."

"I said I wish Len was here and that's when he came into the kitchen and asked me who's Len..."

"And you didn't see him when you went into the kitchen?"

"I already answered that..."

"I need you to answer it again..."

"No – I didn't see him before he came into the kitchen!!"

"What happened after he asked you who's Len?"

"I turned around, I screamed, and I dropped my mug..."

"What happened after that?"

"He told me to clean it up..."

"Did he threaten you?"

"Are you fucking serious right now?!"

"Ms. Cooper –I'm sorry –I know this is difficult – but I have to ask you these questions..."

"I screamed at him to get the fuck outta my apartment and he said he wasn't going to tell me again... and he pointed the gun at me..."

"So he did threaten you..."

"DUH!!"

"Ms. Cooper... please..."

"Yes – he threatened me with his gun!!"

"So you feared for your life..."

"Hell yea – I mean yes – I feared for my life..."

"What happened next?"

"I went to get the broom – he told me don't try anything stupid because he didn't want to have to hurt me..."

"Were those his exact words?"

"Yes..."

"What happened after that?"

"I swept up the pieces of my mug, I put them in the garbage, and then I told him I needed him to leave because I was going to be late for work..."

"What happened after you told him you needed him to leave?"

"He told me he knew I had time for a quickie because I didn't have to leave the house for another 30 minutes..."

"So he's been watching you?"

"He told me he's been watching me..."

"What happened after that?"

"He stood up and said let's go – I told him no..."

"Did he threaten you again?"

"Yes..."

"How did he threaten you?"

"He asked me if he needed to remind me of what's at stake and then he pointed the gun at me again..."

"What happened after he threatened you again?"

"I told him I knew what was at stake; I picked up the pot of coffee, and threw it at him..."

"Did you hit him?"

"Hell yea I hit him – I mean the coffee pot hit him in the head and he was bleeding..."

"What happened after that?"

"He said I was going to regret that and that's when Len said and you're going to regret this and charged at the man..."

"Did you know Len – Leonard – Mr. Allen – was in your apartment?"

"No..."

"What happened after Mr. Allen charged the man that threatened you?"

"They both fell down on the floor... the gun went off... I screamed... Captain Tippet came in... You came in... And you put a gun to Len's head and told him don't move..."

"Okay – here's your statement – look it over – if it's accurate – print your name, sign your name, and date it... Bri took her time going over the statement. She saw that Captain Oddo changed what she said...

"You added something to my statement..."

"I didn't add to your statement – I clarified your statement..." Bri read over the statement again. When she got to the bottom of the statement she read it over slowly...

"They both fell to the floor, the gun went off, and I screamed. Captain Tippet came in and Captain Oddo came in. Mr. Allen was on top of the man that threatened me. Captain Oddo saw Mr. Allen on top of the man that threatened me, he saw the gun on the floor, and he pointed the gun at Mr. Allen. After I screamed it wasn't him, Captain Oddo put his gun down..." Bri looked at Captain Oddo, picked up the pen, and signed the statement...

"Thank you Ms. Cooper – I'll be right back..." he said as he snatched the statement and hurried out the room. Bri got up, left the room, and went towards the main lobby...

CHAPTER 11

"Lieutenant – we might have a problem..." Captain Oddo said as he went to the desk...

"In my office..." Captain Oddo followed the Lieutenant into his office and closed the door... "Did you get her statement?"

"Yes..."

"What's the problem?"

"I added to it..." he explained as he handed the statement to the lieutenant. Lieutenant Fox read the statement and shook his head...

"Did you coerce her into signing this?"

"No sir..."

"Then it shouldn't be a problem – but now that you're here –you can give me your statement...

"Mr. Allen – please tell me what happened – in your own words..." Captain Tippet said as he started writing...

"I wanted to surprise my girlfriend and take her to work..."

"Are you saying Ms. Cooper is your girlfriend?"

"Yes..."

"I need you to say it..."

"Ms. Cooper is my girlfriend..."

"Okay – continue..."

"When I got upstairs, I saw her door was open so I went inside..."

"The door was open?"

"Yes..."

"Okay – continue..."

"I went toward the kitchen and I heard them talking..."

"What did you hear?"

"I heard my girlfriend tell the man he needed to leave because she was going to be late for work..."

"What else did you hear?"

"I heard the man tell my girlfriend she had time for a quickie because she wasn't leaving for work for another 30 minutes..."

"What happened after that?"

"My girlfriend asked the man how he knew that and he told her he'd been watching her..."

"What happened next?"

"He stood up and told my girlfriend let's go and she told him no..."

"What happened after she told him no?"

"He asked her if she needed to be reminded of what was at stake. My girlfriend told him she knew exactly what was at stake; she grabbed the coffee pot, and threw it at him."

"What happened after that?"

"He told my girlfriend she was going to regret that. I told him he was going to regret it, I charged him, I knocked him down on the floor, and the gun went off..."

"What happened after that?"

"You came in, Captain Oddo came in, he pointed a gun at my head and he told me not to move..."

"Did he shoot you?"

"Why the hell are you asking me that?!"

"Because I need an answer..."

"You already know he didn't shoot me!!"

"Please answer the question..."

"No – Captain Oddo didn't shoot me!!"

"Okay – here's your statement – read it over – if it's accurate, print your name, sign it, and date it..." Leonard read over the statement carefully. When he got to the bottom of the statement he read it over twice...

"I was on top of the man that threatened my girlfriend. The gun was on the floor beside him. Captain Oddo pointed the gun at me and told me don't move. He put the gun down after my girlfriend screamed it wasn't me that threatened her..." Leonard looked back at Captain Tippet, picked up the pen, signed the statement, and dated it...

"Thank you Mr. Allen – you can go wait in the lobby..." he said as he took the statement and got up from the table...

"Wait..."

"Yes Mr. Allen?"

"What happens now?"

"We give your statements to our Lieutenant – he takes your statements – the man that threatened your girlfriend gets processed, and everything goes to the D.A...."

"Is there a chance he'll get bail?"

"Not a snowball's chance in hell..." he answered on his way out...

"Lieutenant – I'm ready to give you my statement – oh sorry – I didn't know Oddo was in here..."

"He was just leaving..."

"I'll go check on those fingerprints..." Captain Oddo said as he left the Lieutenant's office...

"Give me the statement..." the Lieutenant commanded...

"Here..." Captain Tippet said as he handed the statement to Lieutenant Fox...

"You better hope they don't say you coerced them into signing these..."

"Lieutenant – I didn't coerce him!"

"I believe you – but the public and the D.A. need to believe you...

"We got it!" Captain Oddo exclaimed as he burst into the office...

"The fingerprints came back?!" Lieutenant Fox asked...

"Yes!"

"Who the hell is this guy?!"

"Benjamin Turner..."

"Ms. Bourequat – thank you for coming in – please come with me..." Captain Tippet said...

"Umm... who are you?" Lina asked...

"I'm sorry – I didn't get a chance to introduce myself I'm..."

"Lina!!" Bri interrupted...

"Bri!!" Lina exclaimed as they hugged...

"Yo – you good?!" Jake asked Leonard as he walked into the main lobby...

"I'm better now – muthafucka's lucky those Captains got there when they did..."

"You're right – you both would've been arrested..." Captain Tippet interjected...

"I'm out – Bri – let's go!!" Leonard snapped as he took Bri's hand and pulled her out the door...

"Len... Wait!!"

"I'm sorry..."

"Are you okay?!"

"Hell no – I was on my way to surprise you· I wanted to take you to work..."

"Oh my God!! I never called out!! Shit!!" she exclaimed as she took out her phone and dialed frantically..."

"Give me that..." Leonard said as he snatched her phone...

"Thank you for calling Courtyard Marriott – can I make a reservation for you?"

"I'm calling for Bri Cooper..."

"She's not in..."

"Yes I know – she's been in an accident..."

"Oh my God!! Is she okay?!"

"She's alright – she was in an Uber and somebody ran right into us – we're on our way to make a report..."

"Can I talk to her?"

"Hold on... Ms. Cooper?"

"Yes?"

"Here – they wanna speak to you..."

94

"Hello?"

"Bri – this is Michelle at the front desk – you alright?!"

"Girl – I'm a little sore – but I'm okay..." she lied...

"Oh no – did you get the license plate?"

"Girl – I didn't get a chance..."

"Oh damn –you going to the hospital?"

"You know what – that's a good idea – I need to make sure I'm okay...'

"Okay girl – take care – I'll see you tomorrow..."

"Well that's just great!!" Bri snapped...

"What's wrong?!"

"I haven't lied that much since I cut class in high school!!"

"That's what you're worried about?!"

"She suggested I go to the hospital – I told her it was a good idea – they're going to want to see papers from the hospital when I go back to work!!"

"Come here..." he said as he pulled her into a hug... "You tell them you went to the emergency room, you saw how crowded it was, you were tired, and you had a headache, so you went home to lie down..."

"So I'm going to lie..."

"Unless you want to tell them the truth..."

"I definitely don't want to do that..."

"Okay then..." he said as he took her by the hand and led her to the car...

"You've done this before – haven't you?" Leonard didn't answer her – he just looked at her and smiled...

CHAPTER 12

"KTLA5 News – this is Gayle Anderson..."

"This is Lieutenant Robert Fox..."

"Good afternoon Lieutenant Fox – what can I do for you?"

"We got him..."

"Who'd you get?"

"We got the serial rapist..."

"Can you give us a statement?"

"I can give you a statement..."

"Thank you Lieutenant – Ellina?"

"Yes Gayle?"

"I need you to get down to Police Headquarters ASAP!!" she exclaimed before she hung up...

"Central..."

"Sherriff Robert – this is Fox..."

"Hey Lieutenant – you got somebody for us or you need somebody?"

"We got him..."

"Who'd you get?"

"We got the serial rapist..."

"No shit! What's his name?"

"Benjamin Turner..."

"Does the press know?"

"Ellina from KTLA5 is on her way down as we speak..."

"Sherriff Robert?"

"Yes Chief Patrick?"

"Benjamin Turner's been processed – he's headed to the infirmary..."

"Thank you Chief...

"I'm sorry about that – I'm Captain Jonathan Tippet – we need to speak with you in private – could you come with me please?" he asked Lina...

"Is she under arrest?" Jake asked...

"Umm... Who are you?"

"I'm Jake Thompson..." he answered as he extended his hand...

"Magic?"

"Yea..."

"I thought you looked familiar – I knew your father..."

"My father knew a lot of people..."

"Why are you here?"

"I asked him to come with me..." Lina answered...

"Hello Ms. Bourequat – I'm Captain Anthony Oddo – thanks for coming in..."

"I'm Jake Thompson..." he said as he extended his hand...

"Why do you look so familiar?"

"That's Magic – Jake's son..." Captain Tippet answered...

"Oh wow! It's so nice to meet you!" Captain Oddo exclaimed...

"Thanks..."

"Magic – I'm sorry, but we need to speak with Ms. Bourequat in private..." Captain Tippet said...

"I'll be right here when you're done..." Jake said as he went to sit down on the bench...

"Thank you for coming in..." Captain Tippet said as they sat down...

"Is this about Bri?"

"No – it's about you..."

"Me?"

"Ms. Bourequat, I run the Robbery, Homicide, & Sexual Assault Division. Captain Oddo runs the Gang & Narcotics Division..."

"Oh my God..."

"We want to talk to you about what happened to you on April 24th this year..."

"I don't want to talk about that..."

"Ms. Bourequat – we need your help..." Captain Oddo said...

"I don't remember what happened..."

"Ms. Bourequat – two women have come forward and filed complaints of sexual assault. Both of these women were taken to El Cholo, had one drink, and they didn't realize what happened until they woke up the next day. They were both treated at the hospital and their bloodwork confirmed that they were drugged..."

"Oh my God... I..." Lina began crying and Captain Tippet gave her his handkerchief...

"We think we can get him off the street – but we need your help..." Captain Tippet said...

"Can't you get him without me?"

"We have a better chance of getting him with your help..."

"I don't want to testify..."

"With your help, we can convince him to skip trial..."

"We've been watching him for a while. He frequents the Elevate Lounge. We believe this is where he gets the drugs..." Captain Oddo said... "We've reviewed surveillance videos from El Cholo. We saw him with the other women and we saw him with you. We'd like you to give us a statement and identify him..."

"I don't want to look at him..."

"You don't have to – we just need you to identify him..." Captain Tippet said as he pushed a photo in front of her...

"That's him..."

"Thank you Ms. Bourequat..."

"Who is he?"

"His name is Kevin Shannon..." Captain Oddo answered...

"I'll give you a statement..."

"Thank you Ms. Bourequat – you can start whenever you're ready...

"I went to a Laker game with my friend Bri..."

"Bri Cooper?"

"Yes..."

"Okay – continue..."

"I met him at the game. He seemed really nice. After the game was over, they offered to take us out...

"They?"

"Yes – Bri met someone too – oh God – was she raped?! Was she drugged too?!"

"Not that we know of..."

"What does that mean?"

"We reviewed the footage from the night you were there and we didn't see anything that would lead us to believe she was drugged by the man she was with..."

"So you're not sure?"

"No..."

"Wait a minute... I just remembered something..."

"What do you remember?"

"When I woke up in the hospital – Bri was there..."

"So she spent the night in the hospital..."

"Yes..."

"Let's get back to what you were saying – you said they offered to take you out..."

"Yes – he asked me where I wanted to go and we both said we love El Cholo..."

"Do you remember anything that happened in El Cholo?"

"I remember we ordered, we ate, we drank... and the next thing I remember is waking up in the hospital..."

"Okay – here's your statement – if it's accurate, print your name – sign it, and date it – oh – one more thing..."

"Yes?"

"We need you to sign a release giving the hospital permission to give us a copy of your records..."

"Okay..." she sighed as she signed her statement and the release...

"Here's our cards – if you can think of anything else – please call us..." Captain Tippet said as he handed Lina their cards...

"Are you okay?" Jake asked when he saw Lina...

"No..." she answered as she started crying...

"What happened?" he asked as he got up to comfort her...

"Let's go..."

"Okay – we can go..."

"I need to go to work..."

"You need to tell me what's going on..."

"Can you take me to work?"

"Will you tell me what's going on?"

"Yes..."

"Okay – where am I going?"

"515 Flower Street..."

"Okay..." When they got there neither of them were prepared for what happened next...

"Oh my God – that's him!!"

"Who?"

"That's the man that drugged me!!"

"I'll fuckin' kill him!!" Jake growled as he started to get out of the car...

"MAGIC!! WAIT!!"

"Give me one good reason why I should wait?!"

"I'm calling the police!!"

"Captain Tippet..."

"This is Lina..."

"Ms. Bourequat?! What's wrong?!"

"He's here!!"

"Where?!"

"My job!!"

"Give me the address!!"

"515 Flower Street!!"

"We're on our way – don't go inside!!"

"Lina – what's going on?!" Jake exclaimed...

"They're on their way – they told me not to go inside..."

"Is that why they wanted to speak to you?!"

"Yes..." They both watched as the police pulled up, they got out the car, and went into the building...

"Good morning – my name is Kevin Shannon – I'm here for an interview with Jennifer Schemerhorn..."

"Good morning – I'm Jennifer Schemerhorn..." she said as she extended her hand...

"Kevin Shannon?" Captain Tippet asked as he walked up on them...

"Yes?"

"You're under arrest..." Captain Oddo said as he put Kevin's hands behind his back and cuffed him...

"Let's go..." Captain Tippet said as they walked him out the building...

"Okay – you're not getting out of this car until I get some answers!!" Jake exclaimed...

"He did this before..."

"Who?!"

"His name is Kevin Shannon..."

"So you knew him?!"

"I didn't find out until this morning..."

"So that's why they wanted to talk to you?!"

"Yes..."

"You said he did this before?!"

"Two women filed a report. They were drugged and raped..." she answered as she started crying...

"Don't cry – I'm sorry..."

"I'm just glad they got him..."

"So am I – but how did they find you?"

"He took them to El Cholo..."

"I still don't understand how they found you..."

"They have surveillance from El Cholo – they saw us having dinner..."

"Us?"

"Me, him, Bri, and the other guy..."

"Oh my God – did she..."

"No – she spent the night with me in the hospital..."

"Why didn't they arrest him after those two women came forward?"

"They wanted me to identify him, they needed me to give them a statement, and they needed me to sign a release for the hospital to give them my records..."

"I still don't understand why he wasn't arrested after those women came forward..."

"They want to get him for drugs..."

"Drugs?"

"Captain Tippet runs the Robbery, Homicide, & Sexual Assault Division. Captain Oddo runs the Gang & Narcotics Division – they've been watching him..."

"Oohhh... Okay..."

"They said he hangs out at Elevate Lounge – they think he gets the drugs there..."

"Why don't you come home with me?"

"I wanna go to work and I wanna check on Bri..."

"Okay – since you don't wanna come home with me – I'll come pick you up from work – and I'll go home with you..."

"Okay..."

"I like that..."

"What?"

"You're smiling..." he answered as he pulled her into a kiss...

"I'll see you later..." she said as she got out the car..."

"I'll be here at 5..." he said as he drove off...

"Lina – you won't believe what just happened!!" Deisy Velazquez exclaimed as she came from behind the desk...

"What happened?!"

"The new hire got arrested before he could be interviewed – you just missed it!!"

"Really?! Wow!!"

"Lina – glad you could make it in – we need to get started on the contract for our new hire – I guess you already heard it won't be Kevin..." Jennifer said as Lina followed her towards her office...

CHAPTER 13

"Central..."

"Sherriff Robert – this is Fox again..."

"Hey Lieutenant – you got somebody else for us or you need somebody else?"

"We got somebody else..."

"Who'd you get?"

"We got Kevin Shannon..."

"The attorney?!"

"Yes..."

"Woo hoo!! Gayle's gonna love this one!!"

"She sure is..."

"Sherriff Robert?"

"Yes Chief Patrick?"

"Kevin Shannon is here..."

"Thanks – Fox – I gotta go – I want Kevin processed and in a cell before the end of my shift – I'll talk to you later...!!"

"Where are we going?" Bri asked...

"Target..."

"Okay..." she sighed. Leonard looked over at Bri and smiled. He was so happy to see her calm and relaxed. Bri closed her eyes as he drove...

"We're here..."

"I need coffee..."

"Will Starbucks do?"

"It'll do..." she sighed as they got out the car and went inside...

"God morning – how may I help you?" the cashier asked...

"I'll have a Venti Caramel Macchiatta..." Bri answered...

"Would you like an extra shot of espresso?"

"Yes sir..."

"Coming right up – can I get you anything sir?" he asked Leonard...

"He'll have what I'm having..." Bri answered...

"What she said..." Leonard laughed...

"Coming right up..." the cashier said as he went to prepare their order...

"I hope I like this..." Leonard said...

"You will – it's espresso, milk, caramel syrup, and whip cream..."

"Sounds sweet..."

"It's not as sweet as you think – I normally have to add sugar to mine..."

"Oh okay..."

"Have you always drank black coffee?"

"No..."

"When did you start drinking black coffee?"

"I don't remember..."

"You don't remember?"

"I had a headache one day – I needed coffee – there wasn't any more milk – I couldn't find the sugar – I've been drinking it black ever since..."

"You didn't think it was nasty?"

"I only thought about getting rid of my headache..."

"Your drinks are ready – you can pay here and pick them up at the end of the counter..."

"Here you go..." Leonard said as he handed the cashier his credit card...

"Thank you..." Bri sighed...

"You're welcome..." Leonard said as the cashier handed him his credit card and they went to the end of the counter to pick up their coffee. Bri watched Leonard as he tasted his coffee...

"What do you think?"

"It's not bad..."

"Good..."

"C'mon – let's go..."

"Where are we going now?"

"To that aisle right over there..." he answered as he pointed towards the aisle marked kitchen appliances and then he grabbed a cart... "Would you like the same color?"

"Same color what?"

"Coffee maker?" Bri burst into tears and Leonard hurried to comfort her...

"I'm sorry – I know how much you like your coffee – I thought..."

"That's very sweet of you..." she sniffed...

"You want us to leave?"

"No – I'd like this coffee maker..." she answered as the pointed to the Mr. Coffee Café Barista coffee maker..."

107

"You got it..." he said as he took it off the shelf and put it in the cart... "Excuse me?" he asked as the salesperson came down the aisle... "What aisle do you have deadbolt locks in?"

"Aisle 13..."

"Thank you..." he said as he took Bri's hand and they went over to the aisle...

"I'm not allowed to change the lock without my landlord's permission..."

"You're not changing the lock – you're adding another lock..."

"He'll want a key..."

"You don't have to give him one..."

"I have to allow him access to the apartment..."

"He has to provide you with notice whenever he needs to access your apartment – when he does, you'll leave the lock open so he can get in – you're not required to allow him 24-hour access to your apartment..."

"Okay..."

"Here's the lock you need..." he said as he picked up the Yale D222 Double Cylinder Deadbolt Lock...

"What if I forget to unlock it when the landlord needs access?"

"He'll have to get over it..." Leonard answered as he put the lock in the cart... C'mon – let's go..."

Bri was quiet in the car. Leonard could see she was deep in thought so he didn't' push her to talk. She continued to sit there after Leonard parked. Leonard got out of the car and opened the door... "C'mon... he said as he extended his hand...

"I'm scared..."

"I know..." Bri took his hand and Leonard helped her out of the car. He closed the door and led her to the entrance...

"I can't go in there..."

"I gotchu..." he said as he put his arm around her. Bri went inside and he followed behind her as she started up the steps. When she got to the top of the stairs, she stopped and turned back to look at him... "I'm right here..." Bri took out her keys, unlocked the door, and went inside. Leonard went in after her and closed the door...

"Where are your tools?"

"Tools?"

"Yes – do you have an electric drill?"

"How'd you know I have an electric drill?"

"Lucky guess..."

"I'll go get it..." Bri went into the kitchen, looked around, and burst into tears. Leonard heard her crying and went to comfort her... "Let's set up the new coffee maker..."

"Okay..." she sniffed. Bri took the old coffeemaker off the counter and put it in the garbage. Leonard put the new coffee maker on the counter and took it out of the box...

"Ooohh... I can't wait to make myself a cup of coffee..." she sighed...

"I'm glad you like it. Are you okay to set it up while I go put this new lock on?"

"Yea..."

"Where's your drill?"

"It's in the bottom drawer near the sink..." she answered as she set up the new coffee maker. Leonard took the drill and went back towards the door. Bri took the broom out of the closet and swept up the broken glass. Leonard put the new lock on the door as she got the Swiffer and cleaned up the dried coffee and blood...

"Bri – come take a look..." Bri threw the dirty Swiffer pad in the garbage and then she went to look at the door...

"It looks good..."

"Here are the keys..." he said as he handed them to her... "You lock it with your key at night when you're inside – you lock it with your key when you leave on the outside..."

"Do I need both keys?"

"No – this lock comes with two keys..."

"I want you to take one of them..."

"Okay..."

"Can this lock be picked?"

"No..."

"Is that it?"

"You're all set..."

"Do you have to go to work?"

"No – I took a personal day..."

"Can you stay with me?"

"I intend to..." he breathed as he pulled her into a kiss. Bri started to walk towards the bedroom and Leonard followed. When they got to the bedroom, she got undressed and got in the bed. Leonard got undressed, got in the bed behind her, and started kissing her on her neck as she started snoring... "Well shit..." he laughed as he spooned her and fell asleep...

"This is Gayle Anderson, News Anchor, KTLA5 News. We interrupt our regularly scheduled programming to bring you this exclusive. Go ahead Ellina...

"This is Ellina Abovian, Reporter, KTLA5 News. Residents in the downtown area can rest easy tonight. We've just confirmed that the Los Angeles Police Department has the armed rapist that has been terrorizing women in Downtown Los Angeles in custody. Lieutenant Fox has confirmed that Benjamin Turner has been arrested and charged with multiple counts of Breaking & Entering, Armed Robbery, First Degree Rape, and Attempted Rape. He is currently being held at Central without bail – back to you Gayle..."

"This is Gayle Anderson, News Anchor, KTLA5 News. We will continue to follow this story and bring you updates. We now return to our regularly scheduled programming..."

CHAPTER 14

"Hey..." Jake sighed as Lina got in the car...

"Hey..." she sighed...

"Bad day?"

"I actually had a good day..."

"You don't sound like you had a good day..."

"I did. When I went upstairs, Deisy told me I just missed the police arresting Kevin..."

"What'd you say?"

"I acted like I was surprised and then Jennifer came to get me before Deisy could continue the conversation..."

"That was rude..."

"It wasn't rude – it was God-sent..."

"Huh?"

"I didn't want to talk about it – God sent Jennifer to come get me so we could get to work – it was exactly what I needed..."

"I guess that's one way to look at it..."

"I love being busy – it makes the day go by quicker – I had this one job where I went into my supervisor's office and I asked her to please give me some work to do because I was falling asleep!"

"Oh shit!"

"I'm glad I don't' work there anymore..."

"Why?"

"I offered to help a few people with some work and I ended up being assigned the work permanently with no extra pay..."

"Typical private sector..."

"I have a lot to do at this job but I don't mind because everyone works hard – and I make more money now than I did when I first graduated from USC..."

"I'm so happy you called the police..."

"Me too – I didn't want you to get arrested!"

"Oh yea – I was definitely going to jail!!" he laughed...

"That's not funny..."

"You're right – I'm sorry..."

"I kinda liked it though..."

"Is that right?"

"Yea – I like how you stood up for me at the station too..."

"What else do you like?" he asked as he took her hand and kissed it..."

"I like the way you make me feel..." Jake smiled a big smile...

"So – since I'm taking you home – what would you like for dinner?"

"I want a shack burger from Shake Shack..."

"You want a shack burger? What if I want to cook for you?"

"You can cook for me when I go back to your house..."

"I'd like that..."

"I wonder how Bri's doing..."

"Call her..."

"Okay..." she said as she dialed her number...

"H... Hello?"

"Hey Bri..."

"Yes Lina?"

"I woke you up – didn't I?"

"You woke us up!!" Leonard yelled in the background...

"I'm sorry – are you hungry?"

"Yea – I haven't eaten all day..."

"We're on our way – I'm stopping at the Shake Shack – I'll call you when we get home..."

"Okay..."

"I like that..." Jake sighed...

"What?"

"You said you'll call her when we get home..."

"Welcome to the Shake Shack – what can I getcha?"

"Four orders – shack burger, fries, two fifty/fifty's, and two kiwi apple limeade..." Lina answered...

"You got it!" the waitress said as she went to place the order....

"What's fifty/fifty?" Jake laughed...

"Oh – that's half lemonade/half organic tea..."

"I thought it was liquor..." he laughed...

You fell asleep on me again..." Leonard breathed as he started kissing Bri on her neck...

"I know... I'm sorry..."

"How much time do we have before they get here..." he breathed as he kissed her...

"Mmm... they stopped... at the... Shake Shack..."

"How much time does that give us..." he breathed as he continued kissing her...

"20... minutes..." she moaned as he spread her legs...

"Here ya go Hunny..." the waitress said as she brought the bags to the counter...

"Here you go..." Jake said as he took his card out and handed it to her...

"Thank you Babe..." she said as she walked over to the register...

"She's very friendly..." Jake laughed...

"She's like that with everybody..."

"Thank God you're not the jealous type..."

"She's married..." Lina laughed...

"Really? Does her husband know how she talks to the customers?"

"Oh yea – sometimes they pretend they're arguing – it's so funny!" Lina laughed...

"Here ya go Babe..." the waitress said as she came back the card and handed it to Jake...

"Thank you Hunny..." Jake said...

"Don't let my husband hear you say that!" she laughed as they both left...

"H... Hello?" Bri answered...

"Did you go back to sleep?"

"Yea..." Bri lied...

"Well c'mon over – we got food..."

"Okay – we're on our way..." Bri said as she hung up. Leonard turned on the television and Bri's mood changed as soon as she saw the news...

"This is Gayle Anderson, News Anchor, KTLA5 News. We interrupt our regularly scheduled programming to bring you this exclusive. Go ahead Ellina...

"This is Ellina Abovian, Reporter, KTLA5 News. Residents in the downtown area can rest easy tonight. We've just confirmed that the Los Angeles Police Department has the armed rapist that has been terrorizing women in Downtown Los Angeles in custody. Lieutenant Fox has confirmed that Benjamin Turner has been arrested and charged with multiple counts of Breaking & Entering, Armed Robbery, First Degree Rape, and Attempted Rape. He is currently being held at Central without bail – back to you Gayle..."

"This is Gayle Anderson, News Anchor, KTLA5 News. We will continue to follow this story and bring you updates. We now return to our regularly scheduled programming..."

"I'm sorry – I shouldn't've turned on the television – I..."

"Stop..." Bri interrupted as she bent down to kiss him...

"Are you okay?"

"I had some good dick – I have a good appetite – and I don't have to cook – yea... I'm okay..."

"Okay then..." Leonard said as they locked the door...

116

"Who is it?" Lina asked...

"Bri..."

"Hold on..." Lina said as she got up to open the door...

"Hey..." Lina said as she pulled Bri into a hug...

"Hey..."

"Hey..." Leonard said as he came in behind Bri...

"Hey!" Ms. Carter said as she came in...

"Ms. Carter – what are you doing here?" Lina asked...

"I was finna' go over there and check on Bri – I saw she was on her way here so I followed her..."

"I'm alright Ms. Carter – thanks for checking up on me..."

"I see you got a new lock on your door – you talk to Henry about that?"

"Who's Henry?" Leonard asked...

"Hello..." Jake said as he came into the living room...

"Henry' the suppa – he's gonna tell the landlord abbot your lock ya know..." Ms. Carter answered...

"I'm not worried about either one of them..." Bri said...

"Whatchall got to eat? Smells good..."

"I'm sorry Ms. Carter – we didn't know you were coming – we had burgers 'n fries..." Lina answered...

"Y'all ain't got nothin' left?"

"No..."

"Okay then – I guess I'll go on home..." she sighed...

"Ms. Carter?"

"Yea Bri?"

"I got a new coffee maker – I'll knock on your door when I get up..."

"You gon' make me a cappuccino?"

"Yea..."

"Okay – don't have me sittin' in my livin' room waitin' – you know I likes to have my coffee with my cigarette..."

"I won't keep you waiting Ms. Carter..."

"Okay... good night y'all..."

"Good night..." they all said in unison...

"Does she always walk up in your house like that?" Jake asked...

"Yea..." Lina laughed...

"She's nosey too – talkin' 'bout she saw Bri so she followed her over here!" Leonard laughed...

"She means well – everybody knows her..." Bri said...

"Does she have any family?" Leonard asked...

"No – her husband died two years ago – we're her family now..." Lina said...

"That's really sweet..." Jake said...

"I think we're the reason she won't go to a retirement home..." Lina said...

"You can take care of yourself..." Jake said...

"She'll be lonely in there – she'll get depressed..." Bri said...

"Aww... you really care about her..." Leonard said...

"Yea..."

"Let's eat!" Lina exclaimed...

"Sounds good to me – especially since I haven't eaten anything all day!!" Bri exclaimed...

"Smells good..." Leonard said...

"We got cheeseburgers, fries, fifty/fifty, and kiwi apple limeade..." Lina said...

"Did you see the news?" Bri asked as Lina took the food and drinks out the bags...

"No..."

"They're talking about the arrest..."

"Oh no – are you okay?"

"I'm getting there. I was scared to go back in my apartment earlier, but Len spent the day with me – he got me a new coffee maker and a new lock for my door..."

"Yea – Ms. Carter was talking about that – what kind of lock is it?" Lina asked...

"It's a deadbolt..." Leonard answered...

"I think you should get one too..." Jake said...

"You think I need one too? Even though he's in jail?" Lina asked...

"Hell yea – you never know what's going to happen..." Leonard said...

"Why don't they have deadbolts on our doors anyway?" Lina asked...

"Because they're expensive..." Jake answered...

"Exactly – they don't do anything unless something happens..." Leonard said...

"Thank you..." Bri sighed as she kissed him...

"You're welcome..."

"I have something to tell you..." Lina said...

"Oh God – do I really need to hear this?" Bri asked as she opened one of the burgers and took a bite...

"Yes..." Lina sighed...

"Okay – I need to eat first – and drink – and then we can talk!" she exclaimed as she took a sip of her kiwi apple limeade...

"This is Gayle Anderson, News Anchor, KTLA5 News. We interrupt our regularly scheduled programming to bring you this exclusive. Go ahead Ellina...

"This is Ellina Abovian, Reporter, KTLA5 News. We've just confirmed that the Los Angeles Police Department has arrested Kevin Shannon, Attorney. Lieutenant Fox has confirmed that Kevin Shannon has been arrested and charged with two counts of rape in the second & third degree, as well as an additional count of attempted rape in the third degree. He is currently being held at Central and bail has been set at $100,000 – back to you Gayle..."

"This is Gayle Anderson, News Anchor, KTLA5 News. We will continue to follow this story and bring you updates. We now return to our regularly scheduled programming..."

"Sherriff Robert – we have a situation!" Chief Patrick exclaimed as he ran into his office..."

"Shit – just as my shift was about to be over – what is it?!"

"It's Benjamin Turner..."

"Oh God – what happened?"

"He's been stabbed – he was rushed to the infirmary – but..."

"Did he make it?"

"He's dead..."

"FUUUCCCKKK!!!"

"Lieutenant Fox..."

"Fox – this is Robert..."

"Yea Fox?"

"Turner was stabbed..."

"Is he dead?"

"Yea..."

"Thanks for letting us know – hopefully we can keep Shannon alive..."

"You want him alive?"

"Hell yea – he'll get more press..."

"Good night..." Sherriff Robert laughed as he hung up...

"Oddo?"

"Yes Lieutenant?" Captain Oddo answered as he came out to the desk...

"Turner's dead..."

"I told him he wasn't going to make it to trial..."

"What's that supposed to mean?!"

"I just meant..."

"Never mind – don't answer that..."

"Damn that was good!!" Leonard exclaimed...

"I thought fifty/fifty was liquor!!" Jake laughed...

"I know – me too!!" Leonard laughed...

"You never ate at the Shake Shack?" Bri laughed...

"Nope..." They both answered in unison...

"You must cook every night..." Lina said...

"I cook one or twice – then I eat leftovers..." Jake said...

"I don't do leftovers..." Bri said...

"Neither do I..." Lina said...

"So what – you eat out all the time?" Leonard asked...

"Naa... we take turns – this way we don't have to deal with leftovers..." Bri answered...

"I guess one of us is going to end up moving..." Jake said...

"Why?" Lina asked...

"Leonard and I don't live close enough to each other for you to take turns cooking..."

"Oh that's okay – we can still take turns – one night I cook – two nights you cook!!" Lina laughed...

"Ohhh – I like that!!" Bri laughed...

"I bet you do!!" Leonard laughed...

"Okay Lina – I'm ready – let me have it..." Bri sighed...

"Okay – remember when Captain Tippet said he was glad I was here this morning?"

"Yea – I was wondering about that..."

"They were coming to see me..."

"Why?"

"They wanted me to come down to headquarters..."

"Yes – I know..."

"No Bri – you don't..."

"Oh God Lina – you too?"

"Bri... remember the night we met those guys after the game?"

"The night you got drunk at El Cholo?"

"Yea..."

"Ooohhh..."

"What am I missing?" Leonard asked...

"I can't tell you... Bri answered...

"Damn – it must be serious..."

"So Bri and I went to a game. We met these guys after the game and they offered to take us out so we said we wanted to go to El Cholo..."

"Le'me find out somebody else took y'all out!" Leonard laughed...

"Len – stop – it's not funny..." Bri said...

"Oh damn – I'm sorry – go ahead..."

"So we went to El Cholo. They seemed really nice..." Jake could see Lina was getting emotional so he put his arm around her... "We ordered food, we ordered drinks, and next thing you know – I woke up in the hospital..."

"Muthafucka..." Leonard mumbled...

"Right!" Jake exclaimed...

"What about Bri?" Leonard asked...

"I was fine – I went with Lina to the hospital and stayed with her all night..."

"I love you Bri..." Lina said...

"I love you too – but why did they want to talk to you?"

"Two women came forward and filed a report..."

"Against them?"

"Not against them – against him..."

"Who's him?" Leonard and Bri asked in unison...

"His name is Kevin... Kevin Shannon... and he's an attorney...

"Oh my God!!" Bri exclaimed...

"The two women that filed a report against him were drugged... and raped..."

"Yo Magic – how the fuck can you sit there so calm?! I'm ready to go kill this muthafucka!!" Leonard exclaimed...

"So was I..." Jake said...

"Was?" Bri and Leonard said in unison...

"They wanted me to give them a statement, identify him, and sign a release so they could get my records from the hospital..." Lina sighed...

"Is he dead?" Bri asked...

"Not yet..." Jake answered...

"That's what the fuck I'm talkin' about!!" Leonard exclaimed... Where the fuck is he?!"

"Wait a minute – you went to the hospital – you didn't file a report – how did they find you?" Bri asked...

"The other women were taken to El Cholo..."

"Oh so this muthafucka has a pattern!!" Leonard exclaimed...

"So they got surveillance from El Cholo... they saw him with them... and they saw him with me..."

"Oh my God... Lina..." Leonard whispered...

"They showed me a picture and told me his name..."

"I should've stayed there – but Len was pissed..." Bri said...

"Yea – I was pissed – I had to leave – sorry about that..."

"She wasn't by herself..." Jake said...

"Thank God..." Bri said...

"They recognized Magic – they said they knew his father..." Lina said...

"Captain Tippet was cool – Captain Oddo didn't wanna speak to me until he found out who I was..."

"They let you go with her?" Leonard asked...

"Naa – I waited in the lobby..."

"So where is he?!" Leonard asked...

"I'm getting to that..." Lina sighed...

"Oh my God – just tell me – I can't take it!!" Bri exclaimed...

"Well... remember I told you I had to get the contract ready for the new attorney that was being hired?"

"Are you fucking serious?!"

"Yea – Kevin was the new attorney..."

"So this muthafucka works at your job?!" Leonard exclaimed...

"Nope..."

"Oh – I was gettin' ready to say!!"

"Magic took me to work and before I could get out the car – we saw him..."

"I didn't know who he was until Lina told me – but after she told me she wouldn't let me get out the car!!"

"Shit – Bri couldn't stop me from getting' out the car!!" Leonard exclaimed...

"She called the police – I'm glad she did – they came and got his ass so I didn't have to..."

"So he's in jail?!" Leonard exclaimed...

"Yea..." Lina sighed...

"Do they know at your job?"

"Nope – I went into work and when Deisy told me what happened I acted like I was surprised..."

"Thank God!!" Bri exclaimed...

"It'll probably be on the news later tonight..." Lina sighed...

"Are you okay?" Jake asked...

"Not really..."

"You want me to stay with you tonight?"

"Yea..."

"Well – we might as well go..." Bri sighed as she got up...

"Are you going to work tomorrow?" Lina asked...

"Yea – why?"

"Cause I'm coming over for coffee..." Lina laughed...

CHAPTER 16

"This is Gayle Anderson, News Anchor, KTLA5 News. We interrupt our regularly scheduled programming to bring you this exclusive. Go ahead Ellina...

"This is Ellina Abovian, Reporter, KTLA5 News. We've just confirmed that Benjamin Turner died in custody. Assistant Sheriff Robert Olmstead has confirmed that Benjamin Turner was attacked in his cell where he was stabbed multiple times. He died while he was being treated in the infirmary. Assistant Sheriff Robert Olmstead has also confirmed they have no suspects at this time. Back to you Gayle..."

"This is Gayle Anderson, News Anchor, KTLA5 News. We now return to our regularly scheduled programming..."

"Hey Bri – good to see you!" Michelle exclaimed...

"Thanks..."

"Alright Bri – have a good day..." Lina said...

"Thanks Lina – you too..."

"Excuse me..." the young woman said as she stopped Lina...

"Yes?"

"My name is Ava – I need to talk to you... and her too..." she said as she pointed towards Bri...

"Who are you?"

"I'm Magic's ex..."

"Well if you're his ex, why do you need to speak to us?" Lina asked as Bri came from behind the counter...

"Hi – I'm Bri Cooper, Manager – Can I help you?"

"My name is Ava – I need to speak to you... and... excuse me – what's your name?"

"My name is Lina..."

"Who are you?" Bri asked...

"I'm Magic's ex..."

"Why do you need to speak to us?" Bri asked...

"Can we do this in private?" Ava asked...

"Sure – we can go in the dining room..." Bri answered as Lina and Ava followed her... "Would you like some coffee?"

"Sure... thanks..."

"Okay – the cups are on the counter along with the milk, sugar, and cream – we have regular and decaf..."

"I'll be right back..." Ava said as she got up to go get a cup of coffee...

"Lord – please don't let me have to beat a Bitch's ass today – I need this job!!" Bri exclaimed...

"Oh God – I hope she doesn't tell me Magic's been sleeping with her behind my back..." Lina sighed...

"Okay... I'm back..." Ava said as she sat down...

"What's this about?" Lina asked...

"I've been wanting to speak to you for a while..." Ava answered...

"Why? Are you sleeping with Magic?"

"I was..."

"Okay – you need to get to the point..." Bri said...

"So we met Magic and Len at a game..."

"Who's we?" Lina asked...

"Me and my friend, Cindy..."

"Okay so?"

"So Magic and I dated for a while – Len ghosted Cindy after he got what he wanted..."

"Wait a minute..." Bri started to say...

"I'm not here to cause trouble – but I need to warn you..."

"Warn us?" Lina asked...

"Magic and Len – they go on the prowl – they stalk women – especially friends – then they hook up with them and dump them..."

"See – first of all –you just said Magic dated you for a while – now you're saying they stalk women and dump them – which is it?" Bri asked. Ava could see Bri was becoming agitated but she continued... "After Len had sex with my friend Cindy - he ghosted her – no call – no text – and when he saw her in the street – he acted like he didn't know her..."

"Look – if Len did that to your friend – I'm sorry – but what does that have to do with us?" Bri asked...

"When they met us – we were at the concession stand and Magic bumped into me and made me spill my soda..."

"Oh my God – maybe Magic is just a klutz!" Lina laughed...

"It happened to you too – didn't it?"

"Yes – Magic bumped into me and made me drop my soda – so what?" Lina laughed...

"They did that on purpose..."

"I doubt that..." Bri said...

"Have you seen Magic's private room?"

"So you've been to his house..."

"Yes – I've been to his house – and I've seen what's in his private room..."

"Yes – computers – he works for the court – that stuff is confidential..." Lina said...

"He told you the same thing he told me..."

"Okay... so?"

"So... one day I got curious... so I went in his private room... and I saw pictures of me all over the walls..."

"Maybe he thought you were attractive!!" Lina exclaimed...

"The pictures were of me in different places... before I met him..."

"Did you confront him?" Bri asked...

"I confronted him – and he broke up with me – he said he couldn't be with a woman that didn't trust him..."

"How long were you dating?" Lina asked...

"Five months..."

"Wow..."

"Lina – she's full of shit!!" Bri exclaimed...

"I wish I were..." Ava sighed...

"Are you sure you're not just hurt because he moved on?" Lina asked...

"Exactly!!" Bri exclaimed...

"Magic seems nice... but there's another side to him..."

"I'll take my chances..." Lina laughed...

"Look Ava – it's been nice talking to you – but I need to get back to work – Lina needs to get to work – have a good day..." Bri said as she got up...

"Here – take my number... Ava said as she tried to hand Bri her number...

"No thank you – bye!" Bri laughed as she walked away...

"Well..." Ava said as she got up... "I guess I'll go..."

"Have a nice day Ava..."

"Be careful with Magic – he's not as nice as you think he is..." she said as she walked out the dining room. Lina got up to leave after Ava left...

"Lina – wait..." Bri said as she went over to her... "You're not worried about what she said – are you?"

"No..."

"You sure?"

"I'm sure..."

"I'ma talk to Len tonight though..."

"I'm talkin' to Magic too - see you later..." she said as she left the hotel...

"Good morning Lina..." Deisy said as she walked in...

"Good morning..." Lina responded...

"Have you seen the news this morning?"

"Not yet – why?"

"Remember that guy I told you about that got arrested yesterday?"

"Yea?"

"He's in the news – hold on – they're running it now...

"This is Gayle Anderson, News Anchor, KTLA5 News. We interrupt our regularly scheduled programming to bring you this exclusive. Go ahead Ellina...

"This is Ellina Abovian, Reporter, KTLA5 News. We've just confirmed that the Los Angeles Police Department has arrested Kevin Shannon, Attorney. Lieutenant Fox has confirmed that Kevin Shannon has been arrested and charged with two counts of rape in the second & third degree, as well as an additional count of attempted rape in the third degree. He is currently being held at Central and bail has been set at $100,000 - back to you Gayle..."

"This is Gayle Anderson, News Anchor, KTLA5 News. We will continue to follow this story and bring you updates. We now return to our regularly scheduled programming..."

Lina ran to the bathroom, locked the door, and burst into tears... "Lina? Are you okay?" Deisy asked...

"I think so – I stopped for coffee and it must've been burnt – it made me nauseous – I'll be out in a minute..." she lied...

"Okay..."

"Central..." Sheriff Robert answered...

"Good morning – do you have a Kevin Anderson in custody?" Lina asked...

"Yes we do..."

"Did he get bail?"

"Yes he did..."

"How much is his bail?"

"Are you going to bail him out?"

"That's depends on how high his bail is..." she laughed...

"His bail was set at $100,000..."

"How much do I need to bail him out?"

"$10,000..."

"Okay thanks..."

"Are you bailing him out?"

"I sure am..."

"May I have your name?"

"I'd rather be anonymous..."

"Fine with me – be here before 5..."

"Can I have his inmate number? I'll be sending the money via Western Union..."

"Sure – his inmate number is 12345-058..."

"Do I send the money to his name?"

"Send the money to Kevin Shannon – Inmate number 1235-058, Men's Central Jail, 441 Bauchet Street, Los Angeles, CA 90002..."

"Thank you so much..."

"You're welcome – as soon as we receive the money – we'll let him know and he'll be out..."

"Thank you..." As soon as Lina hung up, she called her father and proceeded to have a conversation with him in Arabic...

"ya lina! kayf hal 'amirati almaghribiat aljamilati? "

"ya 'abi - 'ana fi wartati!"

"'awh la - ma hu alkhata?!"

"laqad kunt 'ueani - faqadt wazifati - laqad takhalafat ean dafe 'iijariin - watalaqayt liltawi 'ishearan bial'iikhla'i!" bikiti...

"lina ... 'amirati - la tubki ... kam tahtajina?"

"'iijariun hu 2000 dular shhryan - laqad wujidat wazifat 'ukhraa - 'akhbarat malik aleaqar 'anani 'aemal wayumkinuni taewid dhalik - lakinah yurid kula malih bihulul yawm aljumueat 'aw sa'akhruj 'iilaa alshaariei!" bikati...

"lina - 'amirati - la tubki - qul li kam tahtaj ..."

"'abi ... 'iinah kathir!" bikti...

"My Lina - My Princess - faqat qul li kam tahtaj ..."

"'abi - lan 'astatie 'an 'uruda lak ..."

"laqad dafaeat lana bialfiel maratan 'ukhraa min khilal alhusul ealaa shahadatik , walbaqa' ealaa atisal , wa'iirsal al'amwal 'iilayna eindama tastatie - min fadlik qul li kam tahtaj ..."

"'abi ... 'ahtaj 10000 dular ..."

"sa'ursil lak almal baed saea ..."

"shukran lak 'abi..."

"ealaa alrahb walsaeat 'amirati ..."

"ahibk baba..."

"'ana 'uhibuk aydan - tawaqaf ean albuka' - hsnan?"

"hsnan - 'ahtaj 'iilaa aleawdat 'iilaa aleamal - 'iilaa alliqa' ya 'abi ..."

"wdaea ya 'amirati ..."

"My Lina! How is my beautiful Moroccan Princess?"

"Oh Daddy – I'm in trouble!"

"Oh no – what's wrong?!"

"I've been struggling – I lost my job – I fell behind on my rent – and I just got an eviction notice!" she cried...

"My Lina... my Princess – don't cry... how much do you need?"

"My rent is $2,000 a month – I found another job – I told my landlord I'm working and I can catch up – but he wants all his money by Friday or I'm going to be put out into the street!" she cried...

"My Lina – my Princess – don't cry – tell me how much you need..."

"Daddy... it's a lot!" she cried...

"My Lina – my Princess – just tell me how much you need..."

"Daddy – I won't be able to pay you back..."

"You've already paid us back by getting your degree, keeping in touch, and sending us money when you can – please tell me how much you need..."

"Daddy... I need $10,000..."

"I'll send you the money in an hour..."

"Thank you Daddy..."

"You're welcome my Princess..."

"I love you Daddy..."

"I love you too – stop crying – okay?"

"Okay – I need to get back to work – bye Daddy..."

"Bye my Princess..."

"Lina – this is Jennifer – are you okay?"

"I'm okay – I'll be out in a minute..." Lina answered as she turned on the water and began washing her hands. When she was done washing her hands she put her hands under the blower to give herself a few more moments in the bathroom...

"Good thing you answered me – I was getting ready to have Alejandro open the door..." Jennifer laughed...

"Oh my God!!" Lina laughed as they went to her office...

CHAPTER 17

"Hey Lina – I'm going out to lunch – you need me to bring you back anything?" Deisy asked...

"Is it lunch time already?" Lina asked...

"It sure is..."

"Where does the time go?"

"Lina – go ahead – I'll go to lunch when you get back..." Jennifer said...

"Naa – you go ahead – I want to finish this up before I go out – I can wait until you get back..."

"Okay – thanks – we'll see you in about an hour..." Jennifer said as she hurried out the door behind Deisy...

"Good – now I can check my account and see if the money is there..." she said out loud as she checked her account... "Thank you Daddy..." she said out loud as she called her father...

"lina - 'amirati - hal hasalt ealaa almali?"
"neam 'abi!"
"hal tasheur bialsaeadat alan ya 'amirti?"

"'asheur bisaeadat kabirat ya 'abi - shukran lak ..."

"ealaa alrahb walsaeat - 'uhibuk ..."

"ahibuk ayda..."

"walidatuk turid 'an taerif mataa satazuruna ..."

"sati liziaratik qryban ya 'abi - 'aeiduk - lakiniy bihajat lileawdat 'iilaa aleamal ...

"hsnan - 'atamanaa lak ywman seydan ya 'amirati ..."

"'ant aydan ya 'abi ..."

"My Lina – my Princess – did you get the money?"

"Yes Daddy!"

"Are you feeling happy now my Princess?"

"I'm feeling very happy Daddy – thank you..."

"You're welcome – I love you..."

"I love you too..."

"Your mother wants to know when you'll be visiting us..."

"I'll come visit you soon Daddy – I promise – but I need to get back to work...

"Okay – have a good day my Princess..."

"You too Daddy..." she said before she hung up...

"Alright – now I can get back to finishing this before Jennifer gets back..." she said out loud as she went back to her work...

"We're back..." Jennifer said as she came into the office..."

"Okay..." Lina said as she got up to leave..."

"Try to stay cool – it's hot out there..."

"I will..." Lina said as she hurried outside and ordered an Uber...

"Lina?" the driver asked as she got in...

"Yes – I'm Lina..."

"You're going to Western Union?"

"Yes..."

"Alrighty..." Lina didn't talk to the driver as she normally does. She was happy he got her there quickly... "Have a nice day Lina..."

"Thanks – you too..." Lina said as she got out... "Perfect..." she said as she hurried across the street... "Excuse me – miss?"

"Yes?" the young woman answered...

"Can you help me?"

"I don't have any damn money!" the woman laughed...

"My boyfriend's in jail – and I need to bail him out..."

"Girl – how am I supposed to help you with that?"

"I can't go in there – but you can..."

"What you want me to do?"

"Do you have ID?"

"Didn't you see I was about to go in Western Union?"

"I'm sorry – here's what I need you to do – I need you to put your name on this paper – the rest of the information is already filled out..."

"Le'me see that!" the woman said as she snatched the paper... "Oh shit – his bail is $10,000 – you got money like that?!"

"I don't – but he does..." Lina lied...

"Okay – I'll do it for you – but it's gonna cost you..."

"What's that supposed to mean?"

"Well... I was going in here to pay my electric bill – I got a shut-off notice..."

"How much do you need?"

"Well... I'on wanna be greedy or nothin'... but they told me I need to put down at least half..."

"How much is your bill?"

"$500 – I can show you if you don't believe me..."

"I tell you what – I'll give you $500 to pay your electric bill – you go in there and have this money sent to bail my boyfriend out – and when you give me the receipt I'll give you another $100 for your time..."

"Okay! Gimmie the money!" she exclaimed...

"Here you go..." Lina said as she reached in her pocket, took out $500 in folded bills, and put it in her hand...

"I'ma be right back!" the woman exclaimed as she hurried inside. Lina was smiling from ear to ear as she looked in the window and watched the woman pay her electric bill and then hand the cashier the paper to transfer the money. Lina was ready to give the woman the $100 when she came back outside...

"Here's your receipt – you gon' give me another $100 – right?"

"I sure am – thank you so much – I really appreciate you..."

"You welcome!" the woman exclaimed as she made a phone call... "Girl – you not gon' believe this shit!"

"Lina?"

"Magic!"

"What are you doing over here?

"I'm at lunch..."

"They don't have food at Western Union!" he laughed as he pulled up beside her...

"I know – I stopped here to send my father some money..." she lied...

"Aww... that's sweet – do you send them money often?"

"I don't send them money all the time – but I do send them money when I can..." she sighed as she actually told him the truth...

"What time do you need to be back at work?"

"I have another 30 minutes..."

"Do you have time for a quickie?"

"Magic! No!" she laughed...

"I'm talking about getting something to eat – but I like what you're thinking..." he laughed... "C'mon – get in – I'll take you back to work..."

"I didn't get anything to eat..." she sighed...

"I got something for you..." he said as he held up a bag from Shake Shack...

"Oh my God – thank you!"

"You're welcome..."

"How did you know I was at lunch?"

"I went to your job to surprise you and Deisy told me you just left..."

"I'm glad you found me..."

"I'm glad I found you too..." he said as he pulled her into a kiss... "Now let's eat before you have to get back upstairs..." he said as he took the burgers and fries out the bag...

"Excuse me – I need your help..." the woman said as she walked up to Sheriff Robert...

"How can I help you?"

"I'm here to bail out my husband..."

"What's your husband's name?"

"Kevin Shannon..."

"Let me see if we got the money yet..."

"Huh?"

"You called me earlier – I told you as soon as I got the money he'd be out..."

"I didn't call you this morning..."

"What's your name Maam?"

"I'm Mrs. Shannon – Kevin's wife..." she answered...

"Well – according to my screen · $10,000 just posted to his account – he can be released in a few minutes..."

"Oh thank God!"

"Patrick?"

"Yes Sherriff?"

"I need you to go get Kevin Shannon – he made bail..."

"You got it..."

"Shannon?"

"Yes Chief?" Kevin answered...

"Let's go – you're getting outta here..." he answered as he opened the cell...

"I don't understand – where am I going?"

"Hell if I know – Nor do I care – you made bail – let's go!"

"Okay!!" Kevin exclaimed as he followed Chief Patrick to be processed. When the Chief brought him out into the main lobby and he saw his wife, he started to cry..."

"Oh my God – you bailed me out – I love you so much!" he cried as he ran to hug her..."

"I love you too – but I didn't bail you out..."

"If it wasn't you – who was it?"

"I don't know and I don't care – let's get the hell outta here!" his wife exclaimed as she took his hand and pulled him out the door...

"Lieutenant Fox..."

"Fox – this is Robert..."

"Yea Fox?"

"You're not going to believe this..."

"What now?"

"Shannon made bail..."

"That doesn't surprise me – he's a lawyer – they always have money..."

"I got a call this morning from a woman asking if she could bail him out via Western Union..."

"He probably had somebody do that for him so we can't track where the money came from..."

"The crazy thing is his wife just came in here to bail him out too..."

"He's having an affair – his mistress bailed him out..." Fox laughed...

"You know what – I didn't even think of that..." Robert laughed...

"Alright Robert – I gotta go – getting' busy in here – I'll call Gayle..."

"Okay Fox – talk to you soon..." Robert said as he hung up...

"This is Gayle Anderson, News Anchor, KTLA5 News. We interrupt our regularly scheduled programming to bring you this update. Earlier we reported that Kevin Shannon had been arrested and charged with two counts of rape in the second & third degree, as well as an additional count of attempted rape in the third degree. Lieutenant Fox has confirmed that Kevin Shannon has been released and is currently out on bail awaiting trial. We will continue to follow this story and bring you updates. We now return to our regularly scheduled programming..."

"I guess I better get back upstairs..." Lina sighed...

"I love you Lina..." Jake breathed as he pulled her into a kiss...

"I love you too Magic..." she breathed as she kissed him again...

"I love that..." he sighed...

"What?"

"You're smiling..." Lina continued smiling as she got out the car and went back to work...

CHAPTER 18

"Hey Len – can you meet me after work?"

"Sure Bri – is everything okay?"

"Yes..."

"You sure?"

"I'm sure..."

"Okay – what time do you get off tonight?"

"6 o'clock..."

"Okay – I'll see you then...

"Hey Bri..."

"Hey Lina – can you come by here when you get off work?"

"Sure – is everything okay?"

"Everything's okay – but I want us to tell them about Ava..."

"Oh boy – I hope they don't get mad..."

"Why would they be mad at us?"

"I don't know..."

"I get off at 6..." Bri said as she hung up...

"Hey Beautiful..." Jake answered...

"Hey..."

"What's wrong?"

"Bri wants us to meet her after work..."

"That's nice – are we going out?"

"Maybe..."

"What's wrong Lina?"

"We have something to tell you..." she sighed...

"Are you breaking up with me?"

"Never..."

"Okay then – she works at the Courtyard Marriott right?"

"Right..."

"Okay – I'll pick you up and we'll go to the hotel..."

"She gets off at 6..."

"That's fine – I'll see you later..."

"Hey Bri..." Lina said as she walked in...

"Hey Lina, hey Magic – make yourselves comfortable – I need to get back to the front desk..."

"There you are!" Leonard exclaimed as he pulled Bri into a kiss...

"Len – I'm still at work..." she laughed...

"When did this happen?" Michelle asked...

"Mind ya business!" Bri laughed...

"Okay girl – I see you – he's fine!"

"I'll be over there..." Leonard laughed as he went to sit down with Lina...

"Hey..." he said as he sat down with Lina and Jake...

"Hey Len..." Lina said...

"Hey Lina..." Jake looked over at Lina and watched her closely. He could tell she was deep in thought and it had him worried...

"Okay – I'm off the clock!" Bri exclaimed...

"Listen – it's Friday night – it's been a rough week – why don't we go to Takami for dinner and then go to the Elevate Lounge?" Jake asked...

"We really need to talk to you..." Lina sighed...

"Girl – we can talk to them tomorrow – let's hurry up and get outta here – I'm definitely ready to get my eat & drink on!!" Bri exclaimed...

"Okay..." Lina sighed. She wasn't smiling and Jake didn't like it one bit...

"Welcome to Takami – table for four?"

"Yes Maam!!" Bri exclaimed...

"Right this way..." the hostess said as she motioned for them to follow her... "How'd this?" she asked as she brought them to a table...

"Perfect!!" Bri exclaimed as Leonard pulled out a chair for her to sit down and Jake pulled out a chair for Lina to sit down...

"The waitress will be right over..." she said as she went to seat another couple...

"Welcome to Takami – can I start you off with something to drink?" the waitress asked...

"I'll have water – I'm going to drink plenty later..." Bri laughed...

"Make that a pitcher of water for the table..." Leonard said...

"How 'bout some appetizers?"

"Tacos!" Bri and Lina answered in unison...

"Japanese Tacos – anything else?"

148

"Scallops on the half shell..." Leonard said...

"Excellent choice..."

"Softshell crab..." Jake said...

"I'm ready to order my entrée!" Bri exclaimed...

"I'll go put in your appetizers and then I'll be right back..." the waitress said as she left to put in their order...

"How was your day?" Leonard asked...

"Long!" Bri answered...

"How did Ms. Carter like her coffee?"

"I've created a monster..." she sighed...

"She wants to come over every morning – doesn't she?" Leonard laughed...

"She did – but I took care of that..." Bri laughed...

"You did? How?"

"I told you she can't come over when you're there..." she laughed...

"That was a good one!" Leonard laughed...

"I bet she asked you what days he comes over!" Lina laughed...

"You know she did!" Bri exclaimed as they all laughed...

"Here are your appetizers..." the waitress said as she began setting them on the table along with plates...

"Ooohhh... these look so good!" Lina exclaimed. Jake was happy to see Lina smile a little but he knew something was wrong...

"Are you ready to order your entrees?" the waitress asked...

"I'll have the seared tuna!" Bri exclaimed...

"I'll have the grilled salmon..." Leonard said...

"I'll have the chicken teriyaki..." Lina said...

"I'll have the grilled angus filet..." Jake said...

"Will that be white rice or brown rice?"

"White rice!" they all answered in unison...

"Grilled vegetables or steamed vegetables?"

"Steamed vegetables!" they all answered in unison...

"Okay – I'll be back when your foods ready..."

"Oh my God – I hope we have room for the entrees... I'm so full..." Lina said...

"I'm sure you'll have room..." Jake said...

"Here are your entrees..." the waitress said as she put the good on the table...

"Thank you..." Jake said as they started eating...

The sun was starting to go down and they were all getting sleepy... "Okay – I'm ready to get my drink on!" Bri exclaimed...

"Let's go!" Leonard exclaimed as he got up and helped Bri up...

"You ready?" Jake asked Lina...

"I'm ready..." she sighed. Jake was relieved when he saw her smile. He got up, helped her up, and they went towards the Elevate Lounge on the other side...

"Woo hoo! That's my jam!" Bri exclaimed as 'Betchall Never Find' blared from the speakers and DJ Beautiee welcomed everyone...

"You're in the Elevate Lounge with DJ Beautiee listening to classic R & B, Hip-Hop, & Reggae!" 'Betchall Never Find' continued blasting through the speakers as Lina started dancing...

"I love this song!" she exclaimed as she pulled Jake onto the dance floor. Jake was happy to see she was happy and wanted to dance...

"What are we drinking ladies?" he asked...

"Tequila!!" they both exclaimed. Jake was relieved that Lina was smiling and having a good time...

"Okay – Don Julio Blanco for the ladies – what are we drinkin'?" Leonard laughed...

"Hennessey XO..." Jake answered...

"Okay player! I see you!" Leonard exclaimed...

"Hello Lina..." Ava said as she walked up on the four of them...

"Ava? What are you doing here?"

"Yes Ava – what ARE you doing here?" Jake asked as he pulled Lina close to him...

"I wanted to introduce you to my husband – Honey – this is Lina..."

"AAAAGGGHHH!!!" he hollered as Lina grabbed the bottle of tequila and busted Kevin upside his head before anyone could react. The bottle hit his head, broke, and covered his head in broken glass mixed with blood...

"STAY THE FUCK AWAY FROM ME!!" she screamed...

"OH MY GOD?! WHAT THE HELL IS WRONG WITH YOU??!!" Ava screamed...

"Ask your fuckin' husband!!" Jake gritted...

"C'mon – let's get the hell outta here!!" Leonard exclaimed as he hurried Bri out and Jake followed with Lina...

"What are we going to do now?" Bri exclaimed...

151

"We're going to headquarters..." Jake sighed...

CHAPTER 19

"That's her!!" Ava exclaimed as they walked into the precinct...

"Hold on!!" Captain Tippet exclaimed...

"I want her arrested!! She assaulted me!!" Kevin yelled...

"I'll show you assault muthafucka!!" Jake gritted as he charged towards Kevin...

"MAGIC – DON'T MAKE ME SHOOT YOU!!" Captain Oddo boomed as he put his hand on his taser. Jake stopped but he got close enough for Kevin to feel Jake's breath on his face...

"I WANT HER ARRESTED!!" Ava screamed as she pointed at Lina...

"BITCH – SHUT THE FUCK UP!!" Bri yelled...

"ALRIGHT THAT'S ENOUGH!!" Lieutenant Fox boomed as he came from behind the desk... "Tippet – get them over there – Oddo – get them down to the interrogation room – now!!"

"Yes Sir – guys – please come with me..." Captain Tippet said....

"Where are you taking them? Why aren't you arresting her?!" Ava exclaimed...

"I need you and your husband to come with me..." Captain Oddo said as he motioned for Ava and Kevin to follow him...

"Magic – what the hell is going on?! You're not helping the situation!!" Captain Tippet exclaimed...

"ME?! Why the fuck is he out?!"

"He made bail..."

"Bitch should 'a stayed the fuck away from us – I knew we shouldn't've talked to her!!" Bri exclaimed...

"Am I in an episode of the 'Twilight Zone?'" Leonard asked...

"Am I being arrested?" Lina asked...

"No Ms. Bourequat – you're not going to be arrested – but I need to know what happened..."

"I turned around... he was there... I hit him... Oh God!!" Lina cried...

"Lina...' Jake sighed as he comforted her...

"Wait a minute – he came up to you?"

"His wife came up to introduce that muthafucka to us!!" Bri exclaimed...

"So wait – let me get this straight – Mrs. Shannon approached you at the Elevate Lounge – introduced her husband to you – and you hit him over the head with a bottle?!"

"Yes..." Lina cried...

"How do you two know each other?"

"We don't know that Bitch!!" Bri exclaimed...

"Ms. Cooper – I really need you to calm down – you're not helping..."

"Why are you so angry Bri? Did she do something to you?" Leonard asked...

"Hell yea she did something to me – she did something to both of us!!"

"Look – I really want to get to the bottom of this – but you guys are giving me a headache..." Captain Tippet sighed...

"Maybe if he was still locked up you wouldn't have a headache – and we wouldn't be here..." Jake said...

"Magic – I'm going to let that go out of respect to your father – but don't push it..."

"I'm sorry..."

"Apology accepted – now I need to know what happened – one at a time – Ms. Cooper – I'll start with you..."

"That Bitch – sorry – his wife came to the hotel this morning..."

"Why was she at the hotel?"

"She said she needed to speak to us... about them..." Lina answered...

"Ms. Bourequat – you were there?"

"I was there..."

"Hang on a minute..." he said as he wrote down what they said... "Okay – continue..."

"She stopped me and told me she needed to talk to us – me and Bri..."

"Okay – Ms. Cooper – is that correct?"

"Yeessss!!" Bri answered sarcastically...

"Why the hell did she need to talk to you anyway?" Leonard asked...

"Because I used to date her..." Jake sighed...

"So wait – you dated her?" Captain Tippet asked...

"Yes..."

"I take it things didn't end well..."

"They didn't..."

"I still don't understand why she needed to speak to you..." Leonard said...

"She was 'warning' us..." Bri answered as she put up her fingers to emphasize quotation marks...

"Warning you?" Captain Tippet asked...

"According to her, Len ghosted her friend Cindy after he got what he wanted from her..." Bri answered...

"And Magic stalked her..." Lina added...

"Wait – What?!"

"She said Magic and Len stalk women – she said Magic broke up with her because she went into his private room and he had pictures of her all over the room – and she also told me to be careful with Magic because he isn't as nice as I think he is..." Lina explained...

"Damn Magic – what the hell did you to do her?" Captain Tippet laughed...

"I didn't want her anymore..." he sighed...

"So let me make sure I understand this – Mrs. Shannon approached you both at the hotel to warn you about Mr. Allen and Mr. Thompson – and then she sees you at the Elevate Lounge and introduces you to her husband?!"

"Exactly..." Bri answered...

"And you never met her before today?"

"No!!" Bri and Lina answered in unison...

"Something's wrong with her..." Captain Tippet laughed...

"Exactly!!" Bri exclaimed as they all laughed...

"Why aren't you arresting her?!" Kevin demanded...

"Mrs. Shannon – are you aware of the charges against your husband?!" Captain Oddo asked...

"What's that got to do with that woman hitting my husband with a bottle?"

"I'll be right back..." he answered as he left the room...

"Kevin – what's going on?!" she snapped...

"We dated... briefly..."

"Are you fuckin' kidding me?!" she exclaimed as Captain Oddo came back into the room with a file and a lap top...

"Mrs. Shannon – I'm sorry to have to tell you this..." he sighed...

"Tell me what?!"

"These are the women that filed a report against your husband..." he answered as he showed her their photos..."

"They're lying!!"

"These women went on a date with your husband... he drugged them... he took them home..."

"They're lying!!"

"Here's some surveillance from El Cholo..." he said as he turned the lap top so she could see...

"Oh my God!!" she exclaimed...

"Ava – I can explain – it's not what you think!!"

"Don't bother!! I can't believe I was so stupid!!"

"Mrs. Shannon – I need you to look at this..." Captain Oddo said as he pointed at the lap top. Ava watched in horror as she saw her husband sitting at the table with Lina...

"When was this surveillance taken?!"

"Two months ago..." Captain Oddo sighed...

"You cheated on me?! With her?!"

"Ava – I never slept with her!!"

"The only reason you didn't sleep with her is because she passed out in the restaurant before you got a chance to take her home..." Captain Oddo said...

"Oh my God!! You're a monster!!"

"She passed out because she was drunk!!" Kevin exclaimed...

"Mrs. Shannon – Ms. Bourequat woke up in the hospital. They found Rohypnol, GHB (liquid ecstasy), and Ketamine (Special K) in her blood..."

"You were going to rape her?!"

"Ava – no – it wasn't like that – I swear!!"

"I can't believe I wanted to bail you out – I wish you never got out – get the hell away from me!!"

"I wanna press charges!!" Kevin exclaimed...

"What you wanna do is get the hell outta this precinct before your bail gets revoked!!" Captain Oddo gritted...

"I can't wait to get the hell away from you!!" Ava exclaimed as she hurried out the room, into the lobby, and ran right into Lina and Bri...

"Oh God – let's get outta here before I hurt her!!" Bri exclaimed...

"BRI – LINA – WAIT!! PLEASE!!" Ava screamed...

"WHAT?!" Bri snapped...

"I had no idea... I'm sorry..." They all stood there stunned...

"Ava – wait!!" Kevin pleaded as she ignored him, walked out the precinct, and Kevin ran out the door behind her...

"Ms. Cooper – if Mrs. Shannon comes anywhere near the hotel – please don't engage – call us immediately..." Captain Tippet said...

"That won't be a problem – she's banned from the hotel as soon as I get back to work..."

"Can we go now?" Leonard asked...

"I'm ready..." Bri answered...

"I'm ready too..." Lina said...

"C'mon – I'll take you home..." Jake sighed...

"You comin'?" Bri asked as she waited in the doorway. Leonard smile at her mischievously and followed her upstairs to her apartment. Jake walked Lina to her building and opened the door for her to go inside...

"Are you coming upstairs?" Jake kissed her before he answered her...

"No – Good night..." Lina began to cry as he got in his car and drove off...

CHAPTER 20

Jake was seething. As much as he wanted to be with Lina, he couldn't be with her – he had to leave because he was too angry. When he got home, he went straight to his office to look for the file he had on Ava... "Here it is..." he said out loud as he opened the folder, looked at the contents, and closed it. He went out the door, locked it, and got back in his car...

"Who is it?!" Ava snapped...

"Magic..."

"What the hell are you doing here?!" she exclaimed...

"Open the door and you'll find out..."

"You must really think I'm stupid!!"

"It doesn't matter what I think Ava..."

"I'm not letting you in..."

"It would be in your best interest to open the door..."

"You promise you won't hurt me?"

"I'm humbled that you'd take me at my word..."

"You still haven't promised me you won't hurt me..."

"I promise you – I won't hurt you..."

"Okay..." she sighed as she opened the door slowly and he rushed the door... "Aaaagghhh!! You promised me you wouldn't hurt me!!" she cried...

"Are you hurt?!"

"I'm scared..."

"You should be..."

"I'm sorry – I didn't know my husband was a monster – I..."

"I didn't come here to talk about your husband – I came here to talk about you..."

"Me?!"

"You never should've done that Ava..."

"I'm sorry..."

"Now Ava..." he breathed as he pulled her close to him and held her... "We both know you're not sorry..."

"I won't do it again – I'll stay away from them – I promise!!" she pleaded as she began shaking...

"I'm not going to hurt you..." he breathed in her ear...

"Please... let me go..."

"I'm not going to kidnap you either..."

"Let go of me... please..." she pleaded as she started crying...

"I have something to show you..." he said as he took the folder out of his jacket and put it on her table...

"What's that?!"

"See for yourself..." Ava opened the folder and looked at all the pictures of herself. When she saw the nude pictures of herself, she panicked...

"Oh my God – how long have you had these?!"

"Apparently I haven't had them long enough..."

"Please... don't post them online..."

"I have no intention of doing that – you should know me better..." he said as she continued to go through the pictures...

"How did you get pictures of my parents?!"

"You tell me..."

"Oh my God – Lina has no idea who you are!!"

"Lina knows me very well... and she loves me..."

"Lina only loves who pretend to be..."

"I came here hoping we could come to an understanding... I guess I was wrong..."

"Oh please – you just want me to keep my mouth shut!!"

"Basically..."

"She deserves to know the part of you that you keep hidden..."

"What makes you think I've hidden anything from her?"

"You haven't changed a bit..." she said as she shook her head back and forth...

"I'll let you in on a secret..." he whispered as he pulled her close to him and held her... "You're right..."

"Magic... please..."

"All you had to do was live your life and let me live mine but no... You couldn't let me live so you have no one to blame but yourself for what happens next..."

"What's that supposed to mean?"

"Someone has to die..." he answered as he picked up the folder off the table, put it back in his jacket, and left...

"Can we talk?" Bri asked...

"I knew it..."

"We can wait if you don't wanna talk..."

"Let's get this over with..." he sighed...

"Is it true?"

"Yes..."

"So you hit it and bounced?"

"I liked Cindy. We went back to her place. One thing led to another – next thing I know – we're fuckin'..."

"So... you left before she woke up?"

"I spent the night. We got up the next morning and she offered to cook me breakfast..."

"That was nice..."

"I thought so too – until she asked me how I felt about moving in with her...

"Moving in?! After only one night?!"

"That scared the shit outta me. I tried to tell her we needed to take things slow but she wasn't trying to hear it..."

"Wow..."

"That's why I never called her or text her. Whenever I saw her in the street, if she tried to talk to me – I went in another direction..."

"I'm sorry you went through that..."

"I'm sorry too – I've never disrespected any woman – and I never will – my father would kick my ass if I ever did..."

"Come here..." she breathed as she pulled him into a kiss...

"I'm sorry..."

"For what?"

"I'm sorry she made you doubt me..."

"I never doubted you – I told Lina she was full of shit..."

"Thank you for that – but I need to ask you something..."

"What?"

"What did I do to make you so sure about me?"

"You're still here..."

"I love you Bri..."

"I love you too..."

"You ready for bed?"

"Yea..." she answered as she got up and went towards the bedroom...

"I'm going to the bathroom – I'll be right there..."

"Okay..." she yawned. Leonard used the bathroom and went back to the bedroom...

"Well shit!!" he exclaimed. Bri was laying face-down on her pillow on her knees with her ass tooted up in the air...

"Magic... It's Lina... Please call me..." she cried as she left a message on his voicemail before she hung up and continued to cry herself to sleep...

Jake parked the car, got out, and went to his door. After he unlocked it, he opened the door and went straight into his backyard. He started a fire in the fire pit, went back into the kitchen, took a beer out of the fridge, picked up the folder, and went back out into the backyard. He waited for the flames to get a little higher, threw the folder into the pit, and watched it burn as he drank his beer. When he was done drinking his beer he got up, went back into the kitchen, put his empty can in the recycle bin, picked up his phone, and played Lina's message...

"Magic... It's Lina... Please call me..."

"Don't cry now Bitch..." he said out loud as he tried to be angry with her but he couldn't. The truth was he wasn't angry with her at all – he was hurt. He turned his phone off, went upstairs, and went to bed...

"Hey Beautiful..." he yawned as he answered his phone...

"Hey... Did I wake you?"

"Not really..."

"Can we talk?"

"Sure..."

"Can you come over?"

"I'll come pick you up..."

"Okay..."

"Hey Lina..." Bri answered...

"Hey..."

"What's wrong?"

"Magic's mad at me..."

"Are you serious?!" she exclaimed as she sat up...

"What's wrong?" Leonard asked...

"It's Lina – she's upset..." Bri answered as she got up out the bed, put on her robe, and went into the kitchen... "What makes you think he's mad at you?" she asked as the turned on the coffee pot...

"I asked him if he was coming upstairs last night and he said no..."

"WHAT?! He didn't stay with you last night?!"

"No..."

"I can't believe he didn't stay with you after everything that happened..."

"Is Len mad?"

"Not at all – you wanna come over for coffee?"

"No – Magic's on his way..."

"Oh okay – I'll talk to you later..."

"Is everything okay?" Leonard asked as he came into the kitchen...

"No..."

"Is Magic with her?"

"No..."

"Hmmm... that's not like him..." he said as he sat down at the table...

"Who is it?"

"Magic..." Lina was happy to hear his voice and Jake was happy to see her when she snatched the door open... "Hey..." she sighed...

"Hey Beautiful..." he said as he went inside and closed the door behind him... "Let's go sit in the living room..."

"Okay..." Lina was feeling anxious and he could sense it. They sat down on the couch and he took a deep breath before he spoke...

"Did you mean it when you told me you love me yesterday?"

"Yes! How can you ask me that?"

"When you called me yesterday you said we have something to tell you..."

"Yes – Bri wanted..."

"Let me stop you right there..."

"Are you mad at me?"

"I'm not mad – I'm hurt... and yes.... I'm a little mad too..."

"Why?"

"You know I'd do anything to protect you – don't you?"

"Yes..."

"So – if you know that – why didn't you tell me what happened when I came to pick you up?"

"I wanted to – but Bri..."

"Lina – listen to me..."

"Okay..."

"I don't give a damn what Bri wanted – this isn't about Bri – this is about me and you..."

"I'm sorry – I thought it would be better if I waited to tell you in person..."

"So why didn't you tell me when I picked you up?"

"Because Bri..."

"Lina – I know that's your best friend – but that shouldn't've stopped you from telling me what happened earlier – I could've done something about it sooner – but you didn't tell me right away so when I found out I was blind-sided..."

"I'm sorry..."

"If you had told me earlier we wouldn't've been there – that could've been avoided – but you didn't tell me so instead of spending a romantic weekend together we spent Friday night at the precinct – you could've been arrested – and I wouldn't've been able to do a damn thing about it..."

"So it's my fault..."

"That's not what I'm saying..."

"What are you saying then?"

"If you had told me when I came to pick you up, we would've addressed it before we went out – but you didn't tell me so I had to handle it as I saw fit..."

"So that's why you said no..."

"Lina – I wanted to be with you last night but I couldn't – I couldn't let her get away with what she did..."

"Oh my God... what did you do?"

"I went to see her..."

"You went to see her? Why?"

"Why do you think I went to see her? She approached you at the hotel – she told you I'm a stalker – she told you to be careful with me – I couldn't let that stand..."

"What happened?"

"She won't bother us again..."

"What about her husband?"

"He wasn't there... but I'ma handle that too..."

"I thought you said no because you didn't wanna be with me..."

"I'm going to say this to you – and I want you to pay attention..." he commanded as he grabbed her by her shoulders... "I... Love... You. I... Want... You. Do you understand me?"

"Yeesss..." she breathed as he pulled her into a kiss. Jake stood up and extended his hand. Lina took his hand; he helped her up off the couch, and led her into the bedroom. He pulled her close to him and she relaxed in his arms as he kissed her passionately. He led her back towards the bed as he opened her robe and pushed it off her shoulders. When they got to the bed, he pushed her down on the bed, got on top of her, spread her legs, and began making love to her...

"You wanna go out to breakfast?" Leonard asked...

"Yea..."

"What's wrong?"

"I'm worried about Lina..." Bri sighed...

"You wanna call her and see if she wants to go out to breakfast?"

"Yea..." she answered as she picked up her phone and called Lina... "Hmmm – she's not answering her phone..."

"Maybe she went back to sleep..."

"I'm going over there..."

"I'm coming with you..."

When they got over there, Bri opened the door to the building... "You comin'?"

"Naa – I'll wait in the car..."

"Okay..." she said as she went upstairs. When she got to Lina's door she was about to knock but she changed her mind...

"MAGIC... MAGIC... HUH... HUH... HUH..."

"LINA... LINA... LINA... FFUUCCKK!!"

"Where's Lina? Why are you smiling? Is everything alright?!" Leonard asked...

"Everything's fine..." Bri sighed...

CHAPTER 21

"Hey Beautiful..." Jake whispered in Lina's ear...

"Hey..." she yawned...

"I need you to get dressed..."

"Okay..." Jake went out into the living room and sat down on the couch to wait for her...

"Bri!!" Leonard exclaimed, jolting her out of her sleep...

"W... What!!"

"Look!!" he exclaimed as he pointed to the television...

"This is Gayle Anderson, News Anchor, KTLA5 News. We interrupt our regularly scheduled programming to bring you this exclusive. Go ahead Ellina...

"This is Ellina Abovian, Reporter, KTLA5 News. We've just confirmed that Benjamin Turner died in custody. Assistant Sheriff Robert Olmstead has confirmed that Benjamin Turner was attacked in his cell where he was stabbed multiple times. He died while he was being treated in the infirmary. Assistant Sheriff Robert Olmstead has also confirmed they have no suspects at this time. Back to you Gayle..."

"This is Gayle Anderson, News Anchor, KTLA5 News. We now return to our regularly scheduled programming..."

"I've never been so happy to hear somebody died as I am right now!!" she cried as Leonard held her...

"Let's go celebrate!"

"No..."

"This is a good thing!!"

"I know – but after what happened last night – I don't want to celebrate anything..."

"Okay – how 'bout this – let's go back to my place – I'll cook for you and then I'll give you dessert..."

"We can do that..." she answered as she got up out of the bed...

"Yo!" Jake answered...

"Where are you?"

"I'm at Lina's – why?"

"We're getting ready to head to my house – you wanna come hang out?"

"That sounds really good – especially after what happened last night..."

"Okay – I need you to do something for me though..."

"You need me to pick up something?"

"Naa – I got everything – I just need you to help me cook..." he laughed...

"I gotchu..." Jake laughed...

"Aiight – I'll see you there..." Leonard said as he hung up...

"Might as well turn on the tv..."

"This is Gayle Anderson, News Anchor, KTLA5 News. We interrupt our regularly scheduled programming to bring you this exclusive. Go ahead Ellina..."

"This is Ellina Abovian, Reporter, KTLA5 News. We've just confirmed that Benjamin Turner died in custody. Assistant Sheriff Robert Olmstead has confirmed that Benjamin Turner was attacked in his cell where he was stabbed multiple times. He died while he was being treated in the infirmary. Assistant Sheriff Robert Olmstead has also confirmed they have no suspects at this time. Back to you Gayle..."

"This is Gayle Anderson, News Anchor, KTLA5 News. We now return to our regularly scheduled programming..."

"Oh my God..." Lina whispered as she started crying...

"Lina... don't cry... he's dead... he can't hurt Bri anymore..." Jake said as he turned off the television and went to comfort her...

"I know... that's not why I'm crying..."

"Why are you crying?"

"Because..." she sniffed... "I wish Kevin was dead too..."

"C'mon – let's get outta here..."

"Where are we going?"

"To make you happy..."

'Okay..." she sighed as she went out the door. Jake locked the door from the inside, pulled it closed, and followed Lina downstairs...

"This is Gayle Anderson, News Anchor, KTLA5 News. We interrupt our regularly scheduled programming to bring you this update. Last night a fight broke out at the Elevate Lounge. KLTA5 is live at Elevate now – go ahead Ellina...

"This is Ellina Abovian, Reporter, KTLA5 News. I'm here at the Elevate Lounge with the owner who has provided us with a video. As you can see in the video, Kevin Shannon was assaulted with a bottle. From this angle, it's unclear who started the fight. The hospital and the police have no comment. At this time, the owner is estimating damages of at least $50,000. Back to you Gayle..."

"This is Gayle Anderson, News Anchor, KTLA5 News. We will continue to follow this story and bring you updates. We now return to our regularly scheduled programming..."

"Where are go going?" Lina asked as Jake drove...

"I already told you..."

"You said we were going to make me happy..."

"So you know where we're going then..." he laughed. Lina didn't ask any more questions. She just smiled and looked out the window as they continued riding for another 30 minutes...

"We're here..." he said as he pulled into the driveway...

"Hmmm – this isn't your house..."

"You're right..." he said as he took her by the hand and led her to the door...

"Who is it?"

"Magic!"

"Hey!" Leonard exclaimed as he opened the door...

"Hey Len..." Lina sighed...

"Hey..." Jake said as they went inside...

"Where's Bri?" Lina asked...

"She's in the backyard..." Leonard answered. Lina hurried out into the backyard to see Bri...

"Did you see the news?" Jake asked...

"Yea..."

"Did Bri see it?"

"She was so happy she cried..."

"I wish that's why Lina cried..." Jake sighed...

"Why was Lina crying?"

"I thought she was crying because she was upset about what happened to Bri – but that wasn't it..."

"Well what was it then?"

"She said she was crying because she wishes Kevin was dead too..."

"Oh damn!!"

"Bri!!" Lina exclaimed as she ran towards her...

"Lina!!" Bri exclaimed as they hugged...

"Magic was right..."

"Right about what?"

Tracy Wilson

"I asked him where we were going and he said we were going somewhere that would make me happy..."

"You sounded pretty happy this morning..."

"What are you talking about?"

"Well – Len wanted to take me out to breakfast and I wanted to see if you wanted to go so..."

"Oh my God!! You heard us?!"

"Yea..."

"I'm so embarrassed!!"

"Oh please – that's nothing compared to the neighborhood knowing Len's name!!" she laughed...

"The whole neighborhood?!"

"Girl – Len has a deck outside his bedroom... and he has a chaise lounge on that deck... and they way he had me calling his name on that deck..."

"Oh my God!! I thought I was a slut for doing it in the pool!!"

"I was embarrassed until Len told me he knew his neighbors' names too!!" Bri laughed...

"So everybody does it!!" Lina laughed...

"I guess so!!" Bri laughed...

"Can I ask you a personal question?"

"More personal than what we're talking about?"

"Kinda..."

"Sure – go ahead..."

"Did you... never mind..."

"Lina – ask me..."

"Did you... do it to Len?"

"Do what?"

"What he did... to you..."

"Are you asking me if I sucked his dick?!" she laughed...

175

"Yea..."

"Yes – now can I ask you a personal question?"

"I haven't..."

"Do you want to?" Lina didn't answer her – she just looked away... "You want to..."

"Yea..."

"Slut!!" she exclaimed as they both laughed...

"I told you I wanted to be more like you!!" Lina laughed...

"Can I ask you something?" Leonard asked...

"Sure..." Jake answered...

"Why didn't you stay with Lina last night?"

"I was too angry..."

"At Lina?"

"At the situation..."

"Man to man – I think you should've stayed with her – she needed you..."

"Well – since you brought this up – I think my girl should've told me what happened earlier instead of listening to your girl..."

"Don't blame Bri for this..."

"I'm not blaming anybody – especially Bri – I get it – when you suggested we go out it was a good idea – she went through a lot – she needed that..."

"I'm glad you understand that..."

"Can you understand how I feel though?"

"How do you feel?"

"If I had known what happened earlier – I would've checked that Bitch as soon as Lina told me..."

"You would've?!"

"Hell yea I would've – but I didn't know – and we wound up at the precinct – Lina could've been arrested – and I couldn't've done shit about it – it's a good thing she wasn't arrested or I might've killed that Bitch!!"

"You went to check her last night – didn't you?"

"Damn right I did..."

"MAGIC?! WHY?!"

"Are you seriously asking me that?!"

"Yes!! What if she called the police?!"

"I wasn't worried about that..."

"Magic – you need to make Lina your priority – fuck Ava!!"

"I did – and I regret it..." he sighed...

"Was her husband there?"

"No – but I'ma handle him when I see him..."

"Lina – did you and Magic talk?"

"Yea..."

"Where was she last night?"

"He went to see Ava..."

"Why the fuck did he go see that Bitch?! He should've been with you!!"

"He was angry..."

"At you?!"

"No – but he was a little mad at me though..."

"I knew it!!"

"He said if I told him what happened earlier, we would've addressed it..."

"What does he mean we?! I don't wanna talk to that Bitch?!"

"Magic said he was blindsided so he couldn't protect me. He thought I was going to jail..."

"So he went to check her – I wonder how that went..."

"He said she won't bother us anymore..."

"She better not..."

"Len wasn't mad?"

"Nope..."

"Did you talk?"

"Oh hell yea – I brought that shit up as soon as we got in the house..."

"Is it true?"

"Lina – I told you that girl was full of shit!!"

"I know..."

"Oh so NOW YOU KNOW?! Since when?!"

"Magic told me he loved me yesterday..."

"Aww... Len told me he loved me too!"

"You love him..." Lina sighed...

"And you love Magic..." Bri sighed...

"Damn right she does!!" Jake exclaimed as they brought out the food and drinks. The four of them spent the next couple of hours eating, drinking, laughing, and talking until it started getting dark...

"Well... we better get going..." Jake said as he stood up and stretched...

"You ain't gotta leave – you're welcome to stay..." Leonard said...

"Maybe next time..." Jake said as he stood up and stretched... "C'mon Lina..."

"Good night y'all..." Lina yawned...

"Let me see you out..." Leonard said as he got up...

"Sit – relax with Bri – I know the way out..." Jake laughed...

"Fine – bye!!" Leonard laughed as they went into the house...

"I'm surprised you didn't wanna stay..." Lina said...

"I couldn't stay..."

"Why?"

"Because..." he answered as they got in the car... "I wanna fuck... and you're a screamer..."

CHAPTER 22

"This is Gayle Anderson, News Anchor, KTLA5 News. We interrupt our regularly scheduled programming to bring you this update. Last night a fight broke out at the Elevate Lounge. KLTA5 is live at Elevate now – go ahead Ellina...

"This is Ellina Abovian, Reporter, KTLA5 News. I'm here at the Elevate Lounge with the owner who has provided us with a video. As you can see in the video, Kevin Shannon was assaulted with a bottle. From this angle, it's unclear who started the fight. The hospital and the police have no comment. At this time, the owner is estimating damages of at least $50,000. Back to you Gayle..."

"This is Gayle Anderson, News Anchor, KTLA5 News. We will continue to follow this story and bring you updates. We now return to our regularly scheduled programming..."

"I wonder if Lina's seen this?" Leonard asked out loud...

"Seen what?" Bri asked as she came into the kitchen...

"Look..." Leonard answered as he pointed at the television...

"Oh no... I hope she hasn't seen it – what are you doing?"

"I'm calling Magic..."

"Yo!" Jake answered...

"Where's Lina?"

"She's in the shower..."

"I'm surprised you're not in there with her..." Leonard laughed...

"MAGIC – ARE YOU COMING?!"

"I'll be right there – I'm on the phone!!"

"Listen – whatever you do – don't turn on the television!!"

"Why?! What happened?!"

"KTLA5 is running a story about the fight at Elevate – and Lina's in the video..."

"MAGIC!! C'MON!!"

"Shit – I gotta go – I'll talk to you later!!" Jake exclaimed as he jumped up out the bed and hurried into the shower with Lina...

"There you are!!" she squealed as she threw her arms around his neck...

"Here I am..." he breathed as he kissed her. As happy as he was to be with her, he couldn't help but think about what Leonard said – that is – until Lina changed his mind... "What are you doing?"

"What's it feel like I'm doing?" she asked as she stroked his dick...

"It feels like you want some more of me..." he breathed as he kissed her again. Lina kept you soapy hand on his dick as he pushed her back against the bench. When he got to the bench, he stopped kissing her and sat down... "Straddle me..." he commanded.

"I don't know how..."

"There's two ways you can do it..."

"Okay..."

"You can sit on me and put your legs up with your feet in back of me or on either side of me... or... you can sit on me with your knees bent and put your knees on either side of me..."

"Hmmm... that might hurt my knees – I'm going to sit on you with my feet in back of you..."

"Okay..." Lina sat on Jake's lap and started to put her feet in back of him but it was awkward...

"I gotchu..." he laughed as he held her around her waist...

"Okay... I'm ready..."

"Put your arms around my neck..."

"Okay... Ohhh!" she exclaimed as he thrust himself inside her...

"You okay?"

"Yea..."

"You ready?"

"Yea..." Jake began to kiss her as he moved slowly at first. Once they got into a good rhythm, he went faster and began thrusting harder... "Mmmmm... Mmmmm... Mmmmm... Mmmmm..."

"Mmmph... Mmmph... Mmmph... Mmmph..."

"Mmmmm... Mmmmm... Mmmmm... Mmmmm..."

"Mmmph... Mmmph... Mmmph... Mmmph..."

"Mmmmm... Mmmmm... Mmmmm... Mmmmm..."

"Mmmph... Mmmph... Mmmph... Mmmph..."

182

"Mmmmm...   Mmmmm...   Mmmmm...
Mmmmm..."

"Mmmph... Mmmph... Mmmph... Mmmph..."

"MMMMM!!   MMMMM!!   MMMMM!!
MMMMM!! MMMMM!!"

"MMMPH!! MMMPH!! MMMPH!! MMMPH!!
MMMPH!!" Lina relaxed in his arms as he moved his
hands up her body and held her against him as they
continued kissing...

"That... was... fun..."

"Fun?"

"Yea... Good... and... fun..."

"You wanna do it again?"

"Yes..."

"We can do it every time you come here if you
want..."

"Okay..."

"Let's get you some coffee before I take you
home..."

"I wish I could stay here..."

"I wish you could too – but it's only
temporary..."

"What does that mean?"

"It means what it means..." Jake answered as
he got out the shower. Ava rinsed off and got out the
shower but when she got in the bedroom, Jake was
already downstairs. Lina got dressed, went
downstairs, and went into the kitchen as the smell of
hazelnut creamer hit her nostrils...

"Ooohhh... that smells good..." she sighed...

"Come sit down..." Jake said as he put two
plates of food on the table along with two cups of
coffee...

"Ooohhh... scrambled eggs, fruit, sausage, and potatoes!!" she exclaimed as she sat at the table...

"I've been thinking about what happened Friday night..."

"I'm sorry..."

"No – I'm sorry..."

"For what?"

"I'm sorry I wasn't there for you – I'm sorry I let my anger get the best of me – it won't happen again..."

"That's okay – I still love you..."

"I love you too – and I want to make it up to you..."

"You already have..."

"No I haven't – but I have an idea..."

"What's your idea?"

"Move in with me..."

"What?"

"You heard me Lina..."

"I need to think about it..."

"What's there to think about? We love each other - you wish you could stay – I want you to stay..."

"I still need to think about it..."

"Okay – I'll give you some time to think about it – but don't take too long..."

"I won't..." They finished their breakfast and coffee without speaking. Jake was happy to see Lina was smiling, but he was worried about what she was thinking. Jake got up from the table and put the dishes in the dishwasher...

"You ready to go?"

"Yea..."

"Okay then..." he said as he went to the door and Lina followed. Jake went to open the car door for her and waited for her to get in...

"Thank you..."

"You're welcome..." Jake was feeling a bit more confident that she would say yes but he wasn't 100% confident. Lina took Jake's hand and squeezed it as he drove. He was super excited but he didn't show it... "Well – we're home..."

"We're home..." Lina sighed...

"I'll see you tomorrow..." he breathed as he pulled her into a kiss...

"See you tomorrow..." she sighed. Jake waited for her to go inside and then he drove off and headed straight to the Elevate Lounge...

"How is this my fault?! I'm the one that was assaulted!!" Kevin yelled...

"You were assaulted with good reason – I saw you on the news..."

"This is bullshit!! I came down here to set things straight and you're blaming me!!"

"Look Mr. Shannon – your reputation precedes you – you pay us $50,000 to compensate us for damages or I sue you and you end up paying me a lot more – plus attorney fees..." Jake couldn't believe what he walked in on...

"Fine!! Here's my card – send me the bill and I'll write you a check!!"

"I hope for your sake it doesn't bounce..." the owner said as he took Kevin's card...

"Kevin – right?" Jake asked as he walked up on him...

185

"What the fuck do you want?! Didn't your girlfriend do enough?!"

"Here's your drink..." the waitress said as she put a drink in front of Kevin...

"Here..." Jake said as he handed her his credit card... "I'll pay for his drink and mine..."

"What can I get for your Mr. Thompson?"

"Please – call me Jake..."

"What can I get for you Jake?"

"Hennessey..."

"Yes Sir..." the waitress said as she went to prepare the drink...

"Thanks for the drink..." Kevin said as he got up...

"Kevin – wait..."

"Why? Are you having me arrested?"

"No..."

"Why are you here?"

"I wanna get your side of the story..."

"Yea right!!" he laughed...

"Here's your drink..." the waitress said...

"I'll have another – he's buying..." Kevin said as he sat back down...

"Is that right Jake?" the waitress asked...

"It's fine..."

"Yes Sir..." the waitress acknowledged as she went to make the drink...

"You want my side – I'm gonna give you my side – your girl's a whore!!" Jake's blood began to boil. He took a sip of Hennessey in an attempt to swallow his anger, and took a deep breath...

"What makes you say that?"

"They're all whores!!"

"Let's get back to my girl..."

"I saw her at the game. I started talkin' to her. She asked me what kind of work I do. I told her I was an attorney. I could see the dollar signs in her eyes..."

"You know what – now that I think about it – she sized me up too!" Jake lied...

"See?! I told you!!"

"They wanted to go to El Cholo – and then they tried to order everything on the menu!"

"Exactly!!"

"I tried to get her drunk but she wouldn't drink anymore..."

"Yea – she's a lightweight – she passed out after one drink – damn shame too..."

"How so?"

"How much are you into this girl?"

"We just started dating – waitress – bring him another drink..."

"Thanks man..."

"You're welcome – what were you saying?"

"She's a lightweight – she couldn't handle a simple cocktail..."

"What are you saying?"

"I had no intention of raping your girl – it wasn't like that..."

"What was it like?"

"She wanted me to take her home..."

"If she wanted you to take her home – why give her a cocktail?"

"I take them out – I date them – I treat them with respect – I take them home – they change their mind..."

"So you don't get the pussy..."

"Exactly..."

"So... you give them the cocktail... you take them home... you have your way with them... and they don't remember a thing..."

"Have you had your way with that pretty young thing yet?" Jake couldn't control his anger any longer...

"I'll be right back!!" he gritted as he jumped up, ran to the bathroom, hurried into a stall, and locked the door... "UUUGH!! UUUGH!! UUUGH!! UUUGH!! UUUGH!!" Jake slammed his hand against the wall so hard the manager came out of the stall he was in...

"Excuse me – are you alright?!"

"I'm okay – I just had a little less to eat... and a little too much to drink..." he lied...

"Okay – just checking on ya!"

"Thanks – I appreciate it..." Jake flushed the toilet, came out the stall, and washed his hands as the manager left the bathroom...

"Hey man – I was about to come looking for you!!" Kevin laughed...

"I'm alright – I gotta get in the habit of eating more food before I start drinking..."

"So... you really like this girl?"

"Yea..."

"You think you can get her to drop the charges?"

"I tell you what – if you can get me a couple of cocktails – I'll see what I can do..."

"You're alright Jake!!" Kevin exclaimed as he reached in the inside pocket of his jacket and gave Jake two small bags containing three pills each..."

"Thanks – I gotta get going..."

"You're welcome – and thank you!!"

"Hey listen – you'll be back here Friday night – right?"

"I can't come back here until I write them a check for $50,000..."

"Hurry up and write that check – I'll be back on Friday - Moet's on me!!"

"Okay!! See you Friday!!" Jake couldn't get out of there fast enough...

"I   GOTCHU   YOU   MUTHAFUCKA!!"   he boomed as soon as he got in his car...

CHAPTER 23

"This is Gayle Anderson, News Anchor, KTLA5 News. We interrupt our regularly scheduled programming to bring you this update. Last night a fight broke out at the Elevate Lounge. KLTA5 is live at Elevate now – go ahead Ellina...

"This is Ellina Abovian, Reporter, KTLA5 News. I'm here at the Elevate Lounge with the owner who has provided us with a video. As you can see in the video, Kevin Shannon was assaulted with a bottle. From this angle, it's unclear who started the fight. The hospital and the police have no comment. At this time, the owner is estimating damages of at least $50,000. Back to you Gayle..."

"This is Gayle Anderson, News Anchor, KTLA5 News. We will continue to follow this story and bring you updates. We now return to our regularly scheduled programming..."

"Oh wow!!" Lina laughed as she watched the news... "I can't believe he didn't pass out..." she said out loud as she called Bri...

"Hey Lina..."
"Hey..." she laughed...
"What's so funny?"
"I just saw the news..."
"Are you okay?"
"Yea..." she laughed...
"I thought you'd be upset..."
"Oh – so you saw it already..."
"Yea..."
"When?"
"I saw it earlier this morning..."
"Can you come over?"
"Sure – I'll be there in a few..." Bri answered as she hung up...

"Hey Bri..." Ms. Carter greeted...
"Hey Ms. Carter..."
"I saw that man get killed..."
"Yes he did..."
"Good for his ass!!"
"Right!!" Bri laughed...
"You goin' out?"
"Yea..."
"Say hello to Lina when you see her..." she said as she went back into her apartment...

"Who is it?" Lina asked...
"Bri..."
"Hey..." Lina said as she opened the door...
"Hey..."

"Come sit down... I have something to tell you..." she said as she closed the door and went towards the living room. Bri followed her into the living room and they both sat down on the couch...

"What's wrong Lina?"

"Magic asked me to move in with him..."

"WHAT?!"

"Yea..."

"You don't seem happy..."

"I'm happy... but I have a lot to think about..."

"What's there to think about?!"

"Magic made me breakfast. While we were eating, he apologized to me..."

"Aww..."

"He said he was sorry he wasn't there for me and he also said he was sorry he let his anger get the best of him..."

"Aww damn... he really loves you..." Bri sniffed as she wiped her eyes...

"Yea... he does..."

"So what's the problem?"

"My father..."

"Your father?!"

"I'm his Moroccan Princess. I can do no wrong in his eyes..."

"Ooohhh..."

"I don't know what to do..."

"Well... you could tell Magic the truth..."

"I could... but I'm scared..."

"Scared? What are you scared of?"

"Everything..."

"I don't understand..."

"I don't want my father to know what happened..."

"So don't tell him..."

"I want my parent's to meet Magic... but..."

"You're not married..."

"Yea..."

"I want to move in with him... but I want my father to like him first..."

"What about your mother?"

"I don't have to worry about her so much – besides – she'll go along with whatever my father says..."

"What if your father doesn't like Magic?"

"Then my mother will talk to my father on my behalf..."

"What do you want to do?"

"I love Magic – and I love that he wants me to move in with him – but is he asking me to move in with him because he loves me and he wants us to get married one day or does he want me to move in with him because he wants to protect me?"

"What if he loves you so much he wants to protect you?"

"I guess..."

"Think about it – he wasn't there for you when you needed him. He apologized to you. He wants to make it up to you. He wants to make sure you're protected, so he asked you to move in with him..."

"I wish none of this happened..." Lina sighed...

"I wish it didn't happen either – but it did – my man bought me another coffee maker and bought me another lock for my door – your man asked you to move in with him – seems like a no-brainer to me..."

"I'm sorry Bri – I didn't think about it like that..."

"You don't have to apologize – I just want you to see how much that man loves you..."

"I still need time to think about it..."

"Don't think too long..."

"That's what Magic said..."

"Hey Magic..." Leonard answered...

"Hey..."

"You aiight?"

"Yea..."

"You need me to come over?"

"Yea..."

"I'm on my way..."

"Who is it?" Jake asked...

"Me!!" Leonard laughed...

"Hey..." Jake said as he opened the door...

"We drinkin'?"

"Of course..." Jake answered as he closed the door. Leonard followed him into the kitchen and Jake opened the refrigerator...

"Where'd you find Ole English?" Leonard laughed...

"You know the bodegas have everything!" he answered as he took two 40-ounce bottles out of the refrigerator. Leonard followed him out into the backyard...

"What are we celebrating?"

"I asked Lina to move in with me..."

"WHAT?!"

"Yea..."

"Oh shit! Le'me open this bottle so we can drink to this!!"

"She said she needs to think about it..."

"Ooohhh... I get it..."

"What?"

"You wanted her to say yes right away..."

"Yea..."

"Why?"

"I wasn't there when she needed me..."

"So you want her to move in with you?"

"Yes..."

"Are you sure?"

"She's the one..."

"Oh wow..."

"Yea..."

"You're afraid she's going to say no..."

"Yea..."

"Well... I'm going to say this..."

"I know... go ahead..."

"She might say no..."

"I know..."

"It doesn't mean she doesn't love you..."

"I know..."

"You say that – but do you really know?"

"I don't know..." he sighed...

"She's young..."

"I know..."

"You asked her to move in with you..."

"Yes..."

"What happens after that?"

"I don't understand..."

"Are you just planning to have her move in with you and you just live together?"

"No..."

"What's your plan then?"

"I'm ready to marry her..."

"Okay!!"

"Am I moving too fast?"

"I think so..."

"You do?"

"I'm not ready to get married so yes – you're moving too fast for me – but for you – no..."

"I'm not going to ask her right away..."

"Why not?"

"I want her to move in first..."

"What if she says she's not ready to move in with you? Will you still want to marry her?"

"Yes..."

"So why don't you just propose then?"

"I need to handle a few things first..."

"Magic – don't fuck around and wind up losing the woman you love..."

"I can't let anything come between us..."

"You mean you won't let anyone come between you..."

"Exactly..."

"You get on my fuckin' nerves!!" Leonard laughed...

"I'm giving her my mother's rings..."

"See?! Now I gotta go get Bri a ring!!" Leonard laughed...

"I thought you said you weren't ready to get married?"

"I'm not – but you're proposing to Lina..."

"So?"

"Magic – you know damn well as soon as you propose to Lina – Bri's gonna put pressure on me to propose..."

"Yea... I know..." he laughed...

"I'm just not ready to get married..."

"What's stopping you?"

"I just want to keep dating and see where this goes..."

"You don't have to marry her tomorrow!!" Jake laughed...

"You're one to talk!!" Leonard laughed...

"I'm not going to ask her to marry me until all this shit is handled..."

"You're scaring me..."

"Don't be scared – I'm smarter than they are..."

"What's that supposed to mean?"

"Nothing – forget it..." he answered as he turned up the bottle to his mouth...

"Really Kevin?!" Ava yelled as she opened the door...

"This is still my house..." he slurred...

"You're drunk!!"

"So what?!"

"So we just got this hand-delivered!!" she snapped as she shoved the bill from the Elevate Lounge in his face...

"Damn!! That was fast!!"

"$50,000 – we don't have that kind of money!!"

"I'll take out a loan from my 401k..."

"Unfuckin' believable!! First Magic shows up here – now this!!"

"Who's Magic?"

"Lina's boyfriend..."

"Jake?"

"Yea!!"

"What was he doing here?!"

"He was here Friday night..."

"WHAT?! WHY?!"

"He was pissed off because I warned Lina and her little friend about the two of them..."

"Why the hell would you do that?!"

"I was just trying to look out for them!!"

"Did he threaten you?!"

"Oh please – I pay him no mind..."

"So he did threaten you..."

"He didn't threaten me – wait a minute – how do you know his first name?"

"I was drinking with him..."

"WHAT?! HAVE YOU LOST YOUR DAMN MIND?!!"

"He approached me... he offered to buy me a drink – he actually bought me a few drinks..."

"And you fell for that..."

"It's not what you think..."

"What is it then?!"

"He said he wanted my side of the story..."

"Oh my God – he's going to have you arrested!!"

"No he isn't – in fact – he's going to get that girl to drop the charges..."

"He told you that?! And you believe him?!"

"Yea – why wouldn't I?!"

"Oh my God – I can't!!" she exclaimed as she laughed so hard she was holding her stomach...

"It'll all be taken care of by Friday..."

"What does that mean?"

"Jake asked me to meet him down at the Elevate Lounge Friday night – he's buying a bottle of Moet to celebrate – in the meantime – I'm drunk – I'm going to bed..." he slurred as he went into the bedroom, fell onto the bed, and passed out...

CHAPTER 24

"Hey Beautiful..." Jake greeted as Lina got in the car...

"Hey..."

"Umm... excuse me?!"

"Yes Magic?"

"Where's my kiss?!"

"Right here..." Lina answered as she leaned over and kissed him...

"What's wrong?"

"I can't move in with you Magic..." she sighed...

"Can I ask why?" Lina could tell he was disappointed...

"It's my Dad..."

"You told your father?"

"No..."

"I don't understand...

"I'm not sure my father would approve..."

"Oohhh..."

"Are you mad?"

"No Lina... I'm not mad..." he sighed.

"I'm sorry..."

"You don't have to apologize..."

"I'm just not ready..."

"I understand..."

"Okay..." Jake was quiet on the ride home. He tried to be positive, but he failed...

"Well... we're home..."

"Yea..." Lina sighed...

"So I guess I'll see you tomorrow?"

"You wanna come upstairs?"

"Naa – I need to get home..."

"Okay..."

"I'll see you tomorrow..." he said as he kissed her on the cheek..."

"See you tomorrow – I love you..."

"I love you too..." he said as he drove off. As soon as Lina hung up, she called her mother and proceeded to have a conversation with her in Arabic.....

"lina! tifli! kayf halukami?"

"marhaban 'umiy ..." hamast lina wahi tabki ...

"lina - madha hadatha?"

"qabalt 'ahad ma..."

"la tabdu saeidan ..."

"'ana 'uhibuh ya 'umiy ..."

"hal hu yuhabika?"

"neam al'umu..."

"hsanan ma almushkilatu?"

"talab miniy aliantiqal lileaysh maeah ..."

"yajib 'an takun al'umur jadatan baynakuma ..."

"naeam..."

"hal turid 'an tantaqil lileaysh maeahi?"

"neam..."

"'iidhan limadha la?"

"la 'astatbieu..."

"lmaa la?"

"la'anani 'aerif 'ana 'abi lan yuejibah ..."

"lina - la yumkinuk 'an taeish hayatuk bna'an ealaa ma yaetaqiduh waliduk ...

"la 'urid 'an 'ahbitah ..."

"waliduk la yuriduk 'an tahzin ..."

"'abi qal dayman 'iinah yuriduni 'an 'atazawaj ...

"sawf tatazawaj yawman ma ..."

"madha law lam yarghab fi alzawaj mini?"

"hal naqasht hadha maeahi?"

"raqam..."

"lmaa la?"

"la 'uriduh 'an yaghdab ..."

"ealayk 'an tukhbirah bima tasheur bih ..."

"madha law anfasal eani?"

"'iidha anfasal eank , fahu lays alrajul almunasib lak ..."

"'ant ealaa haqin ..." tanahadt lina ...

"kayf hu kulu shay' mae shaqatika?"

"la bi'us..."

"'iidhan 'ant la yatimu tarduka?"

"la 'umiy ..."

"adhhab watahadath maeah ..."

"suf 'umiy ..."

"'ahibuka..."

"'ana 'uhibuk aydan ..." qalat wahi tughliq alkhata ...

"Lina! My Baby! How are you?"

"Hi Mommy..." Lina whispered as she started crying...

"Lina – what happened?"

"I met someone..."

"You don't sound happy..."

"I love him Mommy..."

"Does he love you?"

"Yes Mommy..."

"Well what's the problem?"

"He asked me to move in with him..."

"Things must be serious between you..."

"Yea..."

"Do you want to move in with him?"

"Yes..."

"Then why don't you?"

"I can't..."

"Why not?"

"Because I know Daddy wouldn't like it..."

"Lina – you can't live your life based on what your father thinks...

"I don't want to disappoint him..."

"Your father wouldn't want you to be sad..."

"Daddy always said he wanted me to get married...

"You'll get married one day..."

"What if he doesn't want to marry me?"

"Have you discussed this with him?"

"No..."

"Why not?"

"I don't want him to be mad..."

"You need to tell him how you feel..."

"What if he breaks up with me?"

"If he breaks up with you, then he's not the man for you..."

"You're right..." Lina sighed...

"How's everything going with your apartment?"

"It's fine..."

"So you're not getting evicted?"

"No Mommy..."

"Go talk to him..."

"I will Mommy..."

"I love you..."

"I love you too..." she said as she hung up...

"I'm going to talk to him right now..." she said out loud as she picked up her bag, locked her door, and hurried downstairs...

"Hey Bri..."

"Hey Lina – where are you?"

"I'm in an Uber..."

"You on your way home?"

"I'm on my way to Magic's house..."

"Didn't he pick you up from work?"

"Yea..."

"What happened?"

"I told him I couldn't move in with him..."

"What?! Why?!"

"That's the same thing my mother asked me..."

"Really?"

"Yea..."

"Okay – call me later..."

"I will..." Lina said as the Uber pulled up in front of Jake's house...

"Lina..." he sighed when he saw the Uber pull up in front of his house. He waited for her to get out the Uber and come to the door... "Hey Beautiful..." he greeted as he opened the door...

"Hey – can I come in?"

"Since when do you ask!!" he laughed as he pulled her inside... "What are you doing here?"

"We need to talk..." she answered as she walked into the living room and sat down...

"I thought we already talked..."

"No... We didn't..."

"Okay – let's talk..."

"I called my mother..."

"You did?"

"Yea..."

"How is she?"

"She's good..."

"What made you call her?"

"I called her to talk about you..."

"You told your mother about me?"

"Yea..."

"What did she say?"

"She said I should tell you how I feel..."

"I thought you did..."

"I told you I couldn't move in with you because my father wouldn't approve..."

"I understand that..."

"But I didn't tell you I was scared..."

"I knew that..."

"You did?"

"Of course..."

"I guess my mother was right..."

"About me?"

"Yea..."

"We'll – since you're here – you wanna stay for dinner?"

"If I stay for dinner... I'm not leaving..." Jake just smiled, got up, and went into the kitchen...

"Hey Lina..." Bri answered...
"Hey..."
"You still at Magic's house?"
"Yea..."
"Are you okay?"
"Yea..."
"Hello?? Earth to Lina??"
"I'm sorry – I'm just happy..." she sighed...
"I thought you told Magic you couldn't move in with him?"
"I did..."
"Well I'm glad you're happy..."
"I called my mother..."
"What did your mother say?"
"She said I can't live my life according to what my father thinks..."
"Oh so you changed your mind?"
"No..."
"Well why are you so happy then?"
"Because I told Magic I was scared and he said he already knew that..."
"Oohh..."
"I thought he wouldn't understand..."
"He might understand... but I sure don't..."
"So if Len asked you to move in with him – you'd say yes?"
"Hell yea – but I don't have to worry about that..."
"Why?"
"Because – he's not ready..."
"That doesn't bother you?"

"No – I'm willing to wait until he's ready..."

"What if he's never ready?"

"He loves me – he'll be ready sooner rather than later..."

"I wish I could be more like you..." she sighed...

"Don't worry about being like me – Magic loves you for who you are..."

"Do you ever think about being married?"

"Sometimes..."

"I think about it too..."

"Do you wanna get married?"

"I always wanted to have what my parents have..."

"So do you think you can have that with Magic?"

"I think so – do you think you can have that with Len?"

"Oh yea..."

"Hey Magic..." Leonard answered...

"Guess who's here?"

"Lina?"

"Yes..."

"She said yes?!"

"No..."

"Aww... I'm sorry..."

"I'm not..."

"You're not?"

"When I went to pick her up from work she told me she couldn't move in with me because her father wouldn't approve..."

"You believe that?"

"Oh yea – she's definitely Daddy's little girl..."

"That doesn't bother you?"

"Naa..."

"But she's at your house now?"

"Yes..."

"I'm surprised you didn't take her home..."

"I did..."

"So you took her home – and now she's at your house?"

"Yea..."

"Does she even know what she wants?" Leonard laughed...

"She wants me..."

"Why doesn't she move in with you then?"

"She's scared..."

"That doesn't worry you?"

"Not at all – I just need to convince her that she doesn't have anything to be afraid of..."

"That's not going to be easy..."

"It's not going to be hard either..."

"You're so fuckin' cocky!!" Leonard laughed...

"True – but her mother is actually helping me out..."

"Her mother?! How?!"

"She called her mother when I dropped her off..."

"What did her mother say?"

"Her mother told her she should tell me how she feels..."

"If she's talking to her mother about you, she must really love you..."

"Exactly..."

"You're a lucky man Magic..."

"I'm not the only one..."

"Yea... I'm a lucky man too..."

"I'll call you back later – I'm having dinner with my lady – and if all goes well – I'll be having dessert..."

"I'll talk to you tomorrow..." Leonard laughed as he hung up...

"Kevin! How nice to see you!" the manager greeted...

"Let's skip the pleasantries – here's your damn check!" he snapped as he slammed it down on the bar...

"Thank you for your prompt reply – I trust this isn't going to bounce?"

"Fuck you!!" Kevin exclaimed as he left Elevate Lounge...

"Where did you get the money for the Elevate Lounge?!" Ava snapped as Kevin came in...

"I told you – my 401k..."

"Bullshit – you didn't get the money that fast..."

"What's your point?!"

"My point is you barely left enough money in the account to pay the mortgage!!"

"Weren't you going to bail me out?!"

"What's that got to do with anything?!"

"You're so worried about the mortgage being paid – use some of your money..."

"You arrogant muthafucka!!"

"Oh please – your name's on the mortgage just like mine – it wouldn't kill you to make a mortgage payment..."

"I wouldn't have to make a mortgage payment out of my money if you'd learn to keep your dick in your pants!!"

"You're just mad 'cause I'm giving it to everybody but you..."

"Oh please – why would I want your dick when I can have your partner's dick?"

"What the fuck did you just say to me?!"

"You heard me..."

"You Bitch!!" Kevin exclaimed as he rushed her and grabbed her by her throat... "I should fuckin' kill you!!"

"You have me confused with the Bitches you cheat on me with..." she laughed...

"Keep laughing..." he gritted as he began to squeeze...

"Kevin... I... can't... breathe..."

"That's the idea..." he gritted as he looked in her eyes. Ava just looked back at him with a blank stare until he released his grip...

"Not so funny now – is it?!"

"Enjoy your freedom while you have it!!" she exclaimed as she snatched the door open...

"Where the fuck do you think you're going?"

"Move!!" she exclaimed as she elbowed him in the throat and hurried out the door...

"Ava!! What Happened?!" Barry exclaimed as he opened the door...

"It's Kevin..."she cried...

"I'll fuckin' kill him!!"

"Please... just stay with me..."

"Did he do this to you?!"

"Yes..." she sniffed...

"C'mon – we need to go to the police!!"

"I don't want to go to the police – I just want to stay here – with you..."

"You can't let him get away with this!!"

"He won't – I'll make sure of it..."

"How?!"

"We just had an argument – he pretty much confessed to what he did..."

"WHAT?!"

"He had the nerve to tell me to use the money I was going to bail him out with to pay the mortgage..."

"Muthafucka!!"

"I told him I wouldn't have to pay the mortgage with my money if he'd learn to keep his dick in his pants and he said I was just mad he was giving his dick to everyone but me..."

"WOW!!"

"I'll remember that when I'm called to testify..."

"You may not be able to..."

"Why?!"

"You're his wife – they can't force you to testify against him..."

"They're not forcing me – I'm volunteering – plus – he's also mad because I asked him why would I want your dick when I could have your partner's dick..."

212

"Ava!! Is that why he choked you?!"

"Yea..."

"I'm sorry..." he said as he pulled her into his arms and held her...

"I'm not — now that he said what he said — I can do whatever the fuck I wanna do..." she said as she opened his pants... "And right now..." she said as she dropped down on her knees... "I wanna do you..."

"Ava... Fuuccckkk..." he moaned as she took his dick in her mouth. Barry pulled her up, kissed her hard, and led her into the bedroom...

"Ava..."

"Hmmm?" she yawned...

"It's getting late..."

"So?"

"So I don't want your husband to come looking for you..."

"You don't want me to stay?"

"Of course I do — but if your husband comes looking for you — I can't promise you he'll leave in one piece..."

"As much as I'd like to see that — I'd like him to survive so he can make it to trial..."

"Why do you want him to make it to trial so bad?" Barry laughed...

"Because — as soon as he goes to prison — I get everything..."

"Why don't you just divorce him?"

"I will — but it'll be easier to divorce him after he goes to prison..."

"Ooohhh..."

"He's going to get so many years he won't be able to contest the divorce..."

"So you believe those women are telling the truth?"

"Absolutely..."

"What happened at Elevate?"

"Oh my God..." Ava sighed as she got up out the bed...

"That bad huh?"

"Come with me..." she sighed as they went into the living room...

"What happened?"

"Well – first I tried to be their friend..."

"Their friend?"

"Lina and Bri..."

"Who are they?"

"Lina is dating Magic – Bri is dating his friend, Leonard..."

"You tried to be their friend?"

"I went to the hotel to warn them to be careful – especially with Magic – but they didn't want to hear it..."

"Oh well – fuck 'em..."

"I had put it out of my mind until I saw Lina at Elevate..."

"What happened?"

"I thought I was being nice and cordial by saying hello and introducing her to my husband – that's when all hell broke loose!!"

"Please – tell me what happened!!"

"I thought Lina was a Bitch until I went with my husband to press charges against her..."

"Oh no..."

"Captain Oddo showed me surveillance of my husband with those women... and with Lina..."

"Damn!"

"I felt like such a fool – I apologized to them but they didn't give a damn..."

"I'm sure they don't blame you..."

"This muthafucka had the nerve to tell me he never slept with her – but you went out with her after we got married!!"

"I'm sorry – I can't believe I was in business with him!!"

"Thank God you dissolved the partnership before he ruined you – and here's the kicker..."

"What?"

"He just wrote a check to the owner of Elevate for $50 thousand to cover damages..."

"Why?! He was the one that was attacked!!"

"I'd rather not drag Lina through the mud after what he did to her..."

"Damn..."

"But that's not the end of it..."

"Oh God – what else?!"

"He met Magic there on Sunday – Magic bought him a few drinks – he says Magic wanted his side of the story..."

"And Kevin believed him?!"

"Oh yea – he says they're meeting at Elevate Friday night and Magic's buying a bottle of Moet to celebrate..."

"Celebrate?! Celebrate what?!"

"Kevin actually believes that Magic is going to convince Lina to drop the charges against him!!"

"Even I know better than that!!"

"Exactly – but if Kevin wants to be a fool – who am I to stop him?" she sighed as she got up and stretched...

"That's it – you're staying here for the weekend!"

"Fine with me..." she sighed as she went back towards the bedroom and Barry followed...

"Well hello Kevin..." Jake said out loud as he spotted Kevin downtown... "Where are you going?" Jake followed Kevin and parked across the street as Kevin went into the post office. Kevin came out the post office, got in his car, and headed southwest on North Grand Avenue toward West Temple Street. Jake pulled over and parked when he saw Kevin park, get out, and go into Serendipity Labs on South Grand Avenue... "I sure hope you didn't sign a lease because you aren't going to live long enough to make next month's rent..."

CHAPTER 26

"Jake!!" Kevin slurred when he saw him...

"I see you started without me..." he laughed...

"I couldn't wait to celebrate..."

"I bet..."

"We are celebrating – right?"

"Absolutely..."

"Alrighty then!! Waitress!! Get this man a drink!!"

"Hello Mr. – I mean Jake – it's a pleasure to serve you again tonight..."

"Nice to see you again..."

"Umm... this guy's been drinking for about an hour – he told me to put his drinks on your tab..."

"Muthafucka!!"

"I'm sorry – I thought..."

"Don't worry about it – I told him a bottle of Moet was on me – I guess I took too long to get here..."

"I'm really sorry..."

"Don't worry about it..."

"Thanks – I really appreciate it – I can't afford to get fired..."

"Do me a favor..."

"Sure..."

"Bring me that bottle of Moet..." he said as he slipped a $100 bill in her apron... "And pour two glasses..."

"Yes Sir..." she said as she went to get the bottle of Moet..."

"You still don't have a drink!!" Kevin slurred as he came over to the bar...

"The waitress is getting it for me now – let's get back to the table..." Jake said as he got up from the bar to help Kevin back to the table...

"Ya know – we shouldn't even hav'ta pay for drinks – I just gave them $50,000..."

"Let's forget about that – have you had anything to eat?"

"What're you – my father?" Kevin laughed...

"Would your father offer you a cocktail?" Jake asked as he took one of the bags Kevin gave him out his pocket...

"Oh shit!! I thought you were gonna use that on your pretty young thing!!"

"I did..." he lied...

"How was it?!"

"She was everything I wanted... and more..."

"So you have one left over?!"

"I used the one's you gave me – I liked them so much I went and got more..."

"Oh yea? Where'd you get them from?"

"If I tell ya... I'd have to kill ya..." he laughed...

"Here's your Moet Jake – enjoy!!" the waitress exclaimed as she put the bottle on the table...

"Thanks – bring us some Arane Calamari, Japanese Fries, Zucchini, and Chicken..."

"Yes Sir..." she said as she went to place the order...

"You really are trying to be my father!!" Kevin laughed...

"I just want us to have some food in our stomach so we don't get sick from our cocktails...

"You're crazy!! I'm not taking a cocktail!!" Kevin laughed...

"Oh my God!!" Jake laughed... "I didn't know you were a lightweight!!"

"Who you callin' a lightweight?!"

"You!!"

"I'm nobody's lightweight!!"

"Prove it!!"

"Give me the damn cocktail!!"

"I will – as soon as we get some food in us – in the meantime – let's get some champagne in us before it goes flat..." Jake said as he raised a glass...

"What are we toastin' too?!" Kevin slurred...

"To freedom..."

"TO FREEDOM!!" Kevin exclaimed as he gulped down a glass of Moet...

"To freedom..." Jake repeated as he sipped his glass of champagne...

"And you have the nerve to call me a lightweight – drink up!!"

"Yes Sir!!" Jake exclaimed as he gulped down the glass...

"Here's your food..." the waitress said as she put the food down on the table...

"Bout damn time!!" Kevin exclaimed...

"Thanks – pour us some more champagne – please?" Jake asked as he slipped another $100 bill in her apron...

"Sure..." she said as she poured the glasses...

"Now..." Kevin slurred as he ate... "About that cocktail..."

"Here you go..." Jake said as he gave the little bag to Kevin. Jake smiled a sinister smile as he watched Kevin swallow each pill, taking a gulp of champagne after each pill...

"Okay – your turn..."

"You didn't see me take the cocktail already?!" he lied...

"I must be really drunk..." Kevin laughed...

"You're really drunk... and you're really feeling the effects of your cocktail..." Jake laughed...

"As long as you're not going to try and have your way with me..." Kevin laughed...

"That's exactly what I'm going to do..." Jake laughed...

"You're a funny guy!!" Kevin laughed as he gulped down the rest of the champagne. Jake continued to smile a sinister smile as he finished his glass of champagne...

"How's everything?" the waitress asked as she came to the table...

"We need more champagne!!" Kevin slurred...

"Sir – you've..."

"You heard the man!!" Jake exclaimed as he slipped the waitress another $100 bill...

"Yes Sir!" she exclaimed as she poured two more glasses... "Oh shoot – your bottle's empty..."

"Well what are you waiting for – get us another bottle!!" Kevin slurred...

"Jake?" she asked as she looked over at him...

"You heard the man!!"

"Yes Sir!! She exclaimed as she went to get another bottle of Moet...

"I can't believe I've never had a cocktail before..." Kevin slurred...

"Wait 'till you have another one..."

"Man... you're crazy... you're trying to kill me..." Kevin laughed...

"I'll be right back – I gotta go take a wicked piss..." Jake said as he got up...

"Hang on – I'll go with ya..." he slurred as he stood up and stumbled...

"C'mon... I gotcha..." Jake said as he held Kevin up...

"You're a good guy Jake..." Kevin said as he stumbled towards the bathroom...

"Wow – is he okay?" the manager asked...

"He's fine – he just needs a splash of water on his face... Jake answered as he helped Kevin into the bathroom...

"Oh shit – I gotta pee..." Kevin slurred as he pulled his dick out...

"Wait – let's go in the stall..." Jake said as he pushed Kevin into a stall and locked the door...

"Hey man – what the fuck are you up to?!"

"Oh my God – will you relax?! I'm just in here with you to make sure you don't fall in!!" Jake laughed...

"I'm sorry – le'me hurry up..." Kevin said as he took his dick out and pissed... "Aaaggghhh... that's better..."

"Have you ever been to heaven?"

"Oh hell no – you're gay?"

"What the fuck Kevin?!"

"I'm sorry – I just – never mind – let's go..."

"Have you ever been to heaven?" Jake asked again – this time getting closer...

"Jake – what's going on here?!"

"You take a cocktail... you take a drink..."

"Okay – we did that..."

"You take a second cocktail... you jack off..."

"Oh hell no!!"

"I do it all the time..." Jake said as he put his hand in his pants and pretended to stroke his own dick...

"Jake – Naa – I'm not gay..."

"Here – I saved another cocktail for you..." he said as he handed the little bag to him..."

"I'm not gay man..."

"I'm not gay either – but I already took my second cocktail – and I'm on my way to heaven – with or without you..." he moaned as he continued to pretend he was stroking his dick...

"Gi'me that bag!!" Kevin demanded as he snatched the bag, opened it, and swallowed the pills...

"I'm almost there..." Jake fake moaned...

"I'm on my way..." Kevin panted as he closed his eyes and began stroking his own dick...

"That's it Kevin..." Jake said as he stood there watching... "Join me in heaven..."

"Oh shit – fuck – I'm cummin'..."

"Come with me Kevin..." Jake fake moaned...

"FFUUCCKK!! AAGGHH!!" Jake stood there and watched Kevin slump to the floor...

"Kevin? Are you okay?" he whispered. Jake waited as a few men came into the bathroom...

"Shit – I really gotta go!!" he heard one man say...

"Shut the fuck up and piss!!" another man laughed...

"Fuck you – I'm done!!" the man said as he left the bathroom without washing his hands...

"Nasty muthafucka..." Jake heard the man say as he washed his hands. Jake waited for the door to close before he checked Kevin for a pulse...

"Hmmm – no pulse – I guess you really are in heaven..." he said as he unlocked the door to the stall and came out... "Time to go home..." he said as he went to the sink and washed his hands. Two more men came into the bathroom as he was drying his hands...

"I'm fucked up..." one of them said...

"So am I..." the other one said as Jake left the bathroom...

"Jake – there you are!!" the waitress said as he sat down at the table...

"Here I am..."

"I got you another bottle of champagne as you requested...

"Thanks – but we're done for the night..."

"What about your champagne?"

"Send it to that table over there..." he answered as he pointed to a table full of ladies...

"Yes Sir!!" she exclaimed as Jake got up from the table and left...

CHAPTER 27

"This is Gayle Anderson, News Anchor, KTLA5 News. We interrupt our regularly scheduled programming to bring you this update. We have just confirmed that Kevin Shannon was found unresponsive early Saturday morning in the men's room at the Elevate Lounge. KLTA5 has confirmed that the cause of death was an overdose. KTLA5 is live at Elevate now – go ahead Ellina...

"This is Ellina Abovian, Reporter, KTLA5 News. I'm here at the Elevate Lounge with the manager. The manager issued a statement to the police, stating that he found Kevin Shannon unresponsive in the men's room early Saturday morning and called an ambulance. He was pronounced DOA at the hospital. Back to you Gayle..."

"This is Gayle Anderson, News Anchor, KTLA5 News. We will continue to follow this story and bring you updates. We now return to our regularly scheduled programming..."

224

"Oh my God!!" Ava exclaimed...

"What's wrong?!" Barry asked as he jumped up...

"Kevin's dead!!"

"WHAT?!"

"He's dead!!"

"It's okay Ave – I'm here..." he said as he pulled her into a hug...

"I'm so happy!!" she cried...

"Ava - don't say that..."

"Why not – it's true!!"

"Are you really happy he's dead?"

"Well – if I'm being completely honest – I wanted him to go to prison..."

"So you're not happy he's dead..."

"Oh yea – I'm happy he's dead..."

"Why?"

"No trial – no testimonies – no transcripts – no division of assets – I don't have to deal with any of that – and the best part is this – we all have closure..."

"All?"

"Me, Lina, and the other women..."

"That's true..."

"We can be together as much as we want – we don't have to sneak around anymore – I can invite you over for dinner!!"

"Aren't you worried about what other people will think?"

"I'm not fuckin' other people..." she answered as she straddled him... "I'm fuckin' you..." she panted as she sat on his dick...

"Lieutenant..."

"Yea Tippet?"

"We have a problem..."

"What's wrong?"

"We don't think Kevin died of an overdose..."

"Why not?"

"Here..." Captain Tippet said as he gave Lieutenant Fox the laptop...

"Dammit!! Magic!!"

"I'll call him..." Captain Tippet said as he got up..."

"WAIT!!"

"Yes Lieutenant?"

"Call Ms. Bourequat..."

"Are you sure?"

"Oh yea..."

"Okay..." he sighed as he went into his office...

"Good morning..." Lina answered...

"Good morning Ms. Bourequat – this is Captain Tippet..."

"What can I do for you?"

"Could you come down to the precinct?"

"Why?"

"We have some questions about Kevin Shannon..."

"I already told you everything I know..."

"Have you seen the news?"

"Not yet – why?"

"Ms. Bourequat – Kevin Shannon is dead..."

"Oh my God..."

"Can you come down to speak with us?"

"I guess so..."

"When can we expect you?"

"I'll come down after work..."

"Could you come down this morning?"

"Absolutely not – I'm not taking any time off work for that..."

"Okay – I understand · I'll see you later tonight..." he said as he hung up...

"Is she coming in?" Lieutenant Fox asked...

"Yes..."

"Good – let's get a wire – we need her to start wearing it ASAP..."

"Good luck getting her to wear a wire..." Captain Oddo said as he walked up on their conversation...

"I'll get her to wear a wire..." Lieutenant Fox said...

"Care to place a wager on that?"

"I'm listening..."

"You get Ms. Bourequat to wear a wire – and lunch is on me for a week..."

"I want in on that!" Captain Tippet exclaimed...

"Fine – you guys are going to be buying me lunch for the next two weeks!!" Lieutenant Fox laughed...

"Naa – you're going to be buying us lunch for the next two weeks!!" Captain Tippet laughed...

"Good morning Lina..." Jennifer greeted...

"Good morning..." Lina sighed...

"Did you guys see the news?" Deisy asked...

"I didn't get a chance to watch the news – why?" Jennifer asked...

"Remember that guy Kevin we were about to hire?"

"Deisy – he's no longer relevant – we've already..."

"Look..." Deisy said as she interrupted Jennifer...

"This is Gayle Anderson, News Anchor, KTLA5 News. We interrupt our regularly scheduled programming to bring you this update. We have just confirmed that Kevin Shannon was found unresponsive early Saturday morning in the men's room at the Elevate Lounge. KLTA5 has confirmed that the cause of death was an overdose. KTLA5 is live at Elevate now – go ahead Ellina..."

"This is Ellina Abovian, Reporter, KTLA5 News. I'm here at the Elevate Lounge with the manager. The manager issued a statement to the police, stating that he found Kevin Shannon unresponsive in the men's room early Saturday morning and called an ambulance. He was pronounced DOA at the hospital. Back to you Gayle..."

"This is Gayle Anderson, News Anchor, KTLA5 News. We will continue to follow this story and bring you updates. We now return to our regularly scheduled programming..."

"Oh my God!! I can't believe we were going to hire him!!" Jennifer exclaimed...

"I guess we didn't really know him as well as we thought..." Lina said as she went into her office and closed the door...

"Hey Lina..."

"Hey Bri..."

"Why are you whispering?"

"Have you seen the news?"

"No – why?"

"Kevin's dead..."

"Oh my God!!"

"Captain Tippet wants me to come down to the precinct after work..."

"Why?"

"They have more questions I guess..."

"Why didn't you go this morning?"

"My job doesn't know – and I don't want them to know..."

"Lina?"

"Yes Jennifer?"

"Could you come into my office?"

"I'll be right there!!"

"I'll talk to you later girl – bye..." Bri said as she hung up. Lina got up from her desk and went into Jennifer's office...

"Could you have these depositions copied before lunch? We have a hearing today at 1 p.m...."

"Sure..." Lina answered as she took the depositions and went over to the copier. Lina spent the rest of the morning preparing the folders for the hearing. When she was done, she went back to her office and just as she was walking in, her phone rang...

"Hey Magic..."

"Hey Beautiful – you ready to go to lunch?"

"Sure I'll meet you downstairs..." she answered before she hung up...

"You're going to lunch?" Deisy asked...

"Yea – we have a hearing at 1 p.m. so I need to be back early..."

"Okay – I'll go when you get back – see you later..."

"Hey Beautiful..."

"Hey Magic..." Lina breathed as she leaned over to kiss him...

"Let's go!!" he exclaimed as he drove...

"I can't go too far – we have a hearing today at 1 p.m..."

"Don't worry – I'll have you back on time..." he said as they pulled up in front of Yuko Kitchen... "I'll be right back..." he said as he got out the car. Lina watched him hurry up the stairs and go inside...

"You here for takeout?" the cashier asked...

"Yes – I called in two garlic shrimp rice bowls..."

"Okay – here you go – that's $36.61..."

"Thanks – keep the change..." Jake said as he put $40.00 on the counter and hurried out the door... "Okay – I'm back..." he said as he started the car and drove. When they got to Hancock Park he parked the car and they got out...

"Thanks for bringing me here..." Lina sighed...

"You're welcome..." he said as he took the food out the bag...

"You got us garlic shrimp rice bowls..."

"How'd you know?"

"They smell so good - it's one of my favorites..." They sat there eating and enjoying the breeze until they were finished...

"You ready to go back to work?"

"Yea..." she sighed...

"What's wrong?"

"Nothing – I just wish I could stay here a little longer..."

"We could come back after work if you want..."

"Naaa – I like to come earlier in the day – it gets crowded in the evening..."

"Okay then – let's get you back to work..." he sighed as they got in the car. Lina was quiet on the ride back to work. She didn't lie to Jake about the park getting crowded at night, but the truth was she couldn't go back to the park later because she was meeting with Captain Tippet... "We're back..."

"Yes we are..." she breathed as she pulled him into a kiss...

"I'll see you tonight – I love you..."

"I love you too..." she said as she went back upstairs to her office...

"Perfect timing – he's early..." Deisy said...

"That's fine – go ahead – I'll cover while you're out..."

"Thanks Lina..." Daisy said as she left...

"Ms. Bourequat – thank you for coming in..." Captain Tippet said as Lina walked into the precinct...

"Why am I here?"

"Come with me..." he answered. Lina followed him down the hall to another room where Lieutenant Fox and Captain Oddo were waiting...

"What's going on?" Lina asked...

"Ms. Bourequat – have a seat..." Lieutenant Fox said...

"Okay..." she sighed...

"I'm sorry to have to show you this..." he said as he opened the lap top and hit play...

"Oh my God..." she whispered...

"I'm sorry – we needed you to see this for yourself..."

"What was Magic doing with him?!"

"That's what we need to find out..."

"When was this taken?"

"This was taken Friday night..." Lina continued to watch the surveillance as Jake ate, drank, and laughed with Kevin...

"This can't be right..." Lina whispered as she started crying. Lieutenant Fox gave Lina his handkerchief...

"We hope we're wrong about this..." he said...

"You have to be wrong... he loves me... he wouldn't this to me..."

"I wanna ask you something..."

"Okay..." she sniffed...

"Would you be willing to wear a wire?"

"A wire? Why?"

"I've known Jake all his life. I was friends with his father for many years..."

"Can't you just ask Magic to come down here to explain this?"

"We could – but if we could get him on the wire, it'd be better..."

"Are you trying to arrest him?"

"We're trying not to..." Captain Tippet answered...

"I still don't understand why you need me to wear a wire..."

"I'll be honest – I can't look him in his face and question him..." Lieutenant Fox answered...

"Can I use the bathroom?"

"Sure... You know where it is?"

"Yes - I'll be right back..." she answered as she got up and hurried out the room...

"Why the hell did you let her leave?!" Captain Tippet snapped...

"Trust me – I know what I'm doing..." Lieutenant Fox answered...

"You sure?" Captain Oddo asked...

"Well – we're about to find out..." Lieutenant Fox answered...

"This isn't right... Magic loves me..." Lina cried... "I know you love me Magic... you wouldn't've asked me to move in with you if you didn't..." Lina stopped crying. She used the bathroom, washed her hands, and began smiling to herself as she left the bathroom...

"Are you alright?" Lieutenant Fox asked...

"No..." she lied...

"I know this is difficult..."

"I just can't believe he'd do this to me..."

"We don't wanna believe it either..." Lieutenant Fox sighed...

"Can you show me how to put on the wire?" she sniffed. Captain Tippet and Captain Oddo's eyes got really wide as they were both shocked...

"Are you sure?" Lieutenant Fox asked...

"If Magic really did this to me – he deserves what he gets!!"

"Okay – Tippet – go get the wire..."

"Yes Sir..." Captain Tippet said as he got up to go get the wire. He came back into the office with a box and put it on the table in front of Lina...

"Open the box..." Lieutenant Fox said...

"It's a necklace..." Lina said...

"Take the box home. All you have to do is put the necklace on, record your conversation, and bring the necklace back to us..."

"How will I know it worked?"

"You'll know..."

"Okay..." she sighed...

"You're sure you wanna go through with this?"

"I'm sure..."

"Okay – we'll see you soon..."

"I sure hope you're wrong about Magic..." she sighed as she got up...

"So do we..." Lieutenant Fox said as Lina left...

"You   Son-of-a-Bitch!!"   Captain   Tippet exclaimed...

"I told ya I knew what I was doing!!" Lieutenant Fox laughed...

"I can't believe you actually got her to agree to wear it!!" Captain Oddo exclaimed...

"Well guys – I'm going back out front – I need to get you both a copy of Fleming's menu!!" he laughed as he left the room...

CHAPTER 28

"Well – here goes everything..." Lina sighed as she opened the STTWUNAKE box and took out the contents... "I'm sorry Magic – I hope you'll forgive me..." she sighed. Lina looked up the product on Amazon and watched the video tutorial... "Looks easy enough..." she said as she put the lithium battery in the necklace... "Now let's put this on..." she said as she went over to her dresser and put the necklace on in front of the mirror. Once she was satisfied with how the necklace looked, she called Jake...

"Hey Beautiful..."
"Hey..." she sighed...
"What's wrong?"
"I need to talk to you..."
"You sound upset..."
"I am..."
"I'm on my way..." Lina played with the on/off switch on the necklace as she waited for Jake to knock on the door...

"Who is it?"

"Magic..." Lina made sure the record button was turned on before she opened the door... "Oh my God – what happened?!" he exclaimed as he came inside and closed the door...

"Have you seen the news?"

"Yes..."

"So you know Kevin's dead?"

"Yea..."

"Why didn't you say anything?"

"You were so happy when I came to pick you up for lunch – I didn't want to ruin your day..."

"That didn't work out too well..." she sighed as she started walking towards the bedroom. Jake followed her just as she hoped he would...

"Lina – I'm sorry – I should've told you..."

"That's not what I'm upset about..." she said as she sat down on the bed...

"What is it then?" he asked as he sat down beside her...

"Captain Tippet called me today..."

"What did he want?"

"He said they had questions about Kevin..."

"I thought you told them everything you knew?"

"I thought so too... until they showed me the surveillance..."

"What surveillance?"

"Where were you Friday night Magic?"

"Lina – I can explain..."

"I'm listening..."

"I went to the Elevate Lounge on Sunday..."

"On Sunday?"

"Yes..."

"Why?"

"I wanted to talk to the manager about what happened and Kevin was there..."

"On Sunday?"

"Yes – he was arguing with the manager about the damages..."

"Why didn't you leave?"

"I thought I could get him to trust me – I did it for you..." Lina got nervous...

"What did you do for me?"

"I got him to talk to me..."

"How?"

"I told him I was there to get his side of the story and I bought him a couple of drinks – once he got drunk – he basically told me everything..." Lina sighed with relief when she heard that...

"Why were you there Friday night?"

"When I was there on Sunday, Kevin asked me if I could get you to drop the charges and I told him I'd see what I could do..."

"WHAT?! WHY THE HELL WOULD YOU DO THAT?!"

"I NEEDED HIM TO TRUST ME!! I TOLD HIM TO MEET ME THERE FRIDAY NIGHT SO WE COULD CELEBRATE!!"

"CELEBRATE?! CELEBRATE WHAT?!"

"YOU DROPPING THE CHARGES!!"

"I NEVER DROPPED THE CHARGES!!"

"I KNOW THAT – BUT HE DIDN'T KNOW THAT!! I DID WHAT I DID TO GET HIM TO TRUST ME!!"

"Is that why you were eating, laughing, and drinking with him?!"

"Why else would I be there with that muthafucka?!"

"Oh Magic – I knew you loved me!!"

"Of course I love you..." Jake breathed as he pulled her into a kiss... "I told you... I'll do anything to protect you..." he breathed as they continued kissing... "I even made sure he got to the bathroom..." Lina began to panic. She had to do something to keep him from talking, so she did the one thing she knew she could do to stop him... "Lina – what are you doing?" Lina didn't answer him. She pushed him back on the bed and got between his legs. Jake couldn't see what she was doing and this gave her an opportunity to push the record button to the off position as she snatched the necklace off. When she lifted her head back up, she opened his pants and took out his dick..."

"Lina... Wha..." Lina interrupted him by taking his dick in her mouth...

"FFUUCCKK!!" he moaned as she swirled her tongue on his dick. Jake was in heaven so he had no idea that Lina was terrified she hadn't turned off the recording...

"Come here..." he commanded as he pulled her up towards him and kissed her hard. Lina used this opportunity to snatch the necklace off and stop him...

"Magic – wait..." she panted as she put the necklace in the nightstand and slammed the drawer on it to crack it before she closed the drawer completely...

"Now... where were we?" he growled as he pushed her down on her back and kissed her. Jake pulled up her skirt and when he realized she wasn't wearing any panties, he got really excited... "Why didn't you tell me you were ready for me?" he asked with a crazed look in his eyes...

"I wanted... to... surprise... you... HUH!!" she moaned as he thrust himself inside her... "MAGIC... MAGIC... HUH... HUH... HUH..."

"LINA... LINA... LINA... FFUUCCKK!!"

"HAH!! HAH!! HAH!! HAH!! HAH!!"

"UUGGHH!! UUGGHH!! UUGGHH!! UUGGHH!!" UUGGHH!!" Jake collapsed on top of Lina and kissed her until they both fell asleep...

"LINA?!"

"Huh?"

"WHAT THE FUCK IS THIS?!"

"Magic – I can explain..."

"I love you!! I swore to protect you!! I asked you to move in with me!! And you do this to me?! I thought you trusted me!! How could you do this?!" he asked with tears in his eyes...

"Magic – I can explain..."

"You know what Bitch – FUCK YOU!! I don't ever want to see you again!!" he boomed as he took the STTWUNAKE box, the necklace, and slammed the door on his way out...

"MAGIC!! I'M SORRY!!" Lina cried...

"Magic – what can we do for you?" Lieutenant Fox asked as he came in...

"You can put your head between your legs and suck your own dick!!" he gritted as he slammed the box and the necklace on the counter...

"Magic..."

"Don't bother!!"

"Is there a problem?" Captain Tippet exclaimed as he stormed out of his office to see what the commotion was about...

"FUCK YOU!!" Jake gritted...

"Magic – don't make me..."

"DON'T MAKE YOU WHAT?!"

"Let's talk..." Lieutenant Fox said as he came down from behind the desk...

"There's nothing to talk about!!" Jake gritted as he stormed out...

"Oh shit – he found the wire!!" Captain Tippet exclaimed as Lieutenant Fox called Lina...

"H... Hello?" Lina cried...

"Ms. Bourequat - this is Lieutenant Fox – are you okay?!"

"NOOO!!"

"Did he hurt you?"

"HE DIDN'T HURT ME – I HURT HIM!!" she cried...

"What happened?!"

"He told me everything... I never should've worn that wire..."

"Can you come back down to the precinct?"

"Hell no!!"

"Ms. Bourequat – we wanna help Jake just as much as you do..."

"He called me a Bitch... He said he never wants to see me again..."

"Ms. Bourequat – if you come back down to the precinct – I'll fix this – I promise..."

"You promise?"

"I promise – but I really need you to come back down to the precinct and give us a statement – I can come pick you up if you'd like..."

"Hell no – I'll come to you..."...Lina sniffed as she hung up...

"Is she alright?!" Captain Tippet asked...

"She's alright – she's on her way here to give us a statement..." Lieutenant Fox sighed – here – take this – see if anything can be salvaged..." he said as he handed Captain Tippet the necklace...

"I'll be back..." Captain Tippet said as he took the necklace in his office...

"What was all that about?" Captain Oddo asked as he came in...

"Magic found the wire..." Captain Tippet sighed...

"Oh damn – did we get anything?"

"Naa – he smashed it – we couldn't salvage this if we tried..." Captain Tippet sighed...

"Did we get anything?" Lieutenant Fox asked...

"Naa – he smashed it good – we can't salvage it..."

"Oh well – I might as well place an order..." he sighed as he pulled out the Fleming's menu...

"I can't believe we still have to buy you lunch for two weeks..." Captain Tippet laughed...

"Thank you for coming back..." Lieutenant Fox said as Lina came in...

"Let's get this over with..." she sighed...

241

"Come with me..." he said as she followed him into his office and closed the door...

"Why am I in here?"

"I thought you'd be more comfortable..."

"Oh... okay – what do you need me to do?"

"Just tell me everything he told you..." he answered as he turned on a recorder..."

"You're recording me?"

"Yes..."

"Is that necessary?"

"Ms. Bourequat – I'll take everything you tell me – I'll compare it to the surveillance we have – and then I'll keep my promise to you..."

"You really think you can fix it?"

"I know I can fix it..."

"Okay – I asked..."

"Wait a minute – I need to say this: This is Lieutenant Robert Fox. I'm sitting here with Ms. Lina Bourequat. Ms. Bourequat has voluntarily come into the precinct to give me a statement regarding the death of Kevin Shannon. Go ahead Ms. Bourequat..."

"Okay – I asked Magic where he was on Friday night. He told me he was at the Elevate Lounge on Sunday..."

"On Sunday?"

"Yes..."

"Why?"

"He said he wanted to talk to the manager about what happened and Kevin was there..."

"On Sunday?"

"Yes – he was arguing with the manager about the damages..."

"Why didn't he leave?"

"He said he did it for me..."

"Did what for you?"

"He bought him a few drinks, got him drunk, and got him to talk..."

"Why was he there on Friday?"

"He said they were there to celebrate him getting me to drop the charges..."

"You didn't drop the charges..."

"I know – but Magic said Kevin didn't know that..."

"Did he tell you anything else?"

"Yea – he said he even made sure Kevin got to the bathroom – whatever that means..."

"Can you wait here?"

"Sure..."

"I'll be right back..." Lieutenant Fox said as he got up and left his office...

"Tippet!!"

"Yes Lieutenant?"

"Get me the surveillance from last Sunday at Elevate – and get me the surveillance from Friday again – bring it to my office..."

"Yes Sir..." Captain Tippet said as Lieutenant went back into his office...

"Is everything okay?" Lina asked...

"Hell no..." Lieutenant Fox sighed...

"What's wrong?"

"Based on the statement you just gave me – I think we made a huge mistake..." he sighed as Captain Tippet brought in the surveillance from the Elevate Lounge...

CHAPTER 29

"We need to talk..." Lina said as Jake opened the door...

"I've said all I have to say to you!!" he exclaimed as he tried to slam the door on her but she put her foot in the doorway... "Move your damn foot!!" he gritted...

"As you wish..." she replied as she stepped inside...

"Okay that's it – get out!! Now!!"

"No..."

"Don't make me put my hands on you..." he gritted as he started to push her...

"You can push me out if you want – and I'll leave – but when you open your door I'll be right here..."

"I'll get a restraining order!!" Lina bust out laughing... "I'm not playing with you Lina!! We're fuckin' done!!"

"We're just getting started..."

"What the fuck is wrong with you?! I don't want you here – just go!!"

"Hear me out – after you hear what I have to say, if you still want me to leave – I'll leave – it'll break my heart – but I'll leave..."

"Break your heart?! What about my heart?! How could you do that to me?! How could you betray me?!"

"I didn't do that to you – I did that for you..."

"What the fuck are you talking about?"

"After the way you reacted when we saw Kevin outside my job, I knew you'd do anything to protect me..."

"Yes I would – that's why I don't understand..."

"I'm my father's Moroccan Princess – I can do no wrong in his eyes – so when I called him crying he was very upset..."

"So your father knows what happened?"

"My father knows how much I've been struggling – I'm barely making ends meet – well – that's what I told him to get him to wire me the $10,000 I needed to bail Kevin out..."

"What the fuck?!"

"I told my father I needed money to keep from being evicted. My father said he'd wire me the money. After I got the money, I went to Western Union and I wired the money to Kevin's inmate account number..."

"Why?! Why the fuck would you do that?!"

"I did that because I wanted him dead..."

"So you hired a hitman?!"

"I didn't need to hire a hitman – I had you..."

"Oh my God..."

"I knew what you'd do once he got released on bail..."

"So you set me up – and then you wore a wire to frame me – I should fuckin' kill you!!"

"I didn't wear the wire to frame you – I wore the wire to help you..."

"How the fuck did wearing a wire help me?!"

"If I wanted to frame you, you'd be in jail right now. I had to go along with what they asked me to do so I could convince them I didn't trust you..."

"You don't trust me!!"

"Do you think you found the wire by accident?"

"WHAT?!"

"I wore the wire and gave them just enough to make them think I didn't trust you. When you were getting close to telling me what you did, I found a way to get you to stop talking, I took the wire off, and I put it where I knew you'd find it..."

"So that's why you sucked my dick?"

"That's not the only reason..."

"When I found that wire..." he said as he got choked up...

"I know... I'm sorry..." she said as she got up to comfort him... "I needed you to be angry... I needed you to go confront the Lieutenant – I knew they'd call me to check on me – and I performed when they did..."

"You performed?"

"I cried – I told them how much I hurt you – I knew they'd ask me to come down to give them a statement..."

"You went back to the precinct and gave them another statement?"

"Yes..."

"What did you tell them?"

"I told them the truth..."

"I don't understand..."

"I told them what you told me – and I told them you said you even made sure Kevin got to the bathroom..."

"Oh my God... that might not have been a good idea..." he sighed...

"They'll see you were just helping him because he was drunk – and the manager and the waitress will back you up..."

"How do you know that?"

"I saw the surveillance – remember?"

"I had no idea you had this in you..."

"You weren't supposed to..."

"I don't know if I'm in love with you... or if I'm afraid of you..." he sighed as he shook his head...

"I love you too..." she sighed as she pulled him into a kiss... "What if this isn't over?"

"It's over - Kevin died of an overdose from his own cocktail – C'mon..." he said as he pulled her by the hand towards the room marked 'PRIVATE'...

"What are you doing?"

"I have something to show you..." he said as he opened the door...

"Oh my God!!" she exclaimed as she looked at all the pictures of herself... "How long were you stalking me?!"

"About a month..."

"So... that night... at the game..."

"That was on purpose..."

"So it's true then?!"

"Yes..."

"I was nothing more than a game to you?!"

"You know better than that Lina..."

"How could I have been so stupid?!"

"Don't say that – you're not stupid..."

"I fell for one of the oldest tricks..."

"You didn't fall for a trick – you fell for me!! I'm not a trick – I'm a man – a man that fell in love with you from the moment I saw you – a man that would do anything for you – a man that..."

"Stop talking!!" she interrupted... "Does Len love Bri?! Or was this a game to him too?!"

"He loves her..."

"How do you know he loves her?! I can't wait to..."

"Listen to me!!" he gritted as he pulled her close to him so fast it startled her... "You're not going to tell Bri anything!! You're going to let your friend be happy!!"

"She deserves to know the truth!!"

"The truth is your best friend and my best friend found each other – however it happened – and you're not going to ruin it..." he breathed as he kissed her forcefully. Lina tried to push him away at first but Jake held her tighter so she couldn't get away from him. When she began to relax in his arms, he continued kissing her gently for a few moments... "I have something for you..." he breathed as he led her over to his desk, sat her down in the chair, opened a drawer, and took out an envelope... "Here – open it..." Lina opened the envelope and began to cry...

"Oh Magic..."

"I wanted to surprise you..."

"I can't wait to go see my parents!!" she exclaimed as she jumped up out the chair and threw her arms around him...

"So does that mean you forgive me?"

"Yes..."

"I forgive you too..."

"I won't say anything..."

"Good..."

"I love you so much..."

"Do you love me enough to do what you did to keep me from talking again?" Lina didn't answer him. She pulled him closer, slid his shorts down over his ass, opened her mouth, and swallowed his dick... "FFUUCCKK!!" he moaned as he grabbed her head and pushed his dick in further...

CHAPTER 30

"Who is it?!" Ava snapped...

"Magic..."

"Get the hell away from my door!!"

"I just want to talk..."

"You got what you wanted – my husband's dead – leave me alone!!"

"Okay... I tried..."

"You tried?! Tried what?!" she snapped as the opened the door...

"I haven't tried anything yet..." he answered as he stepped inside...

"Oh my God – get out!!"

"I want to ask you something..."

"You killed my husband – and now you want me to do you a favor?! Have you lost your fuckin' mind?!"

"I didn't kill your husband..."

"Bullshit!!"

"Think about what you're saying..."

"What's there to think about?!"

"Why would I be here if I killed your husband?"

"Because you're a true narcissist..."

"Thank you for the compliment – but I didn't kill your husband and that's not why I'm here..."

"What do you want?!"

"I want the money..."

"What money?!"

"I want the money that got awarded to your husband's estate..."

"Oh my God... you're not only a narcissist... you're a monster..."

"What are you talking about?"

"You killed my husband... and now... you want me to pay you for killing him..." she whispered...

"I didn't kill your husband – and I don't want you to give the money to me..."

"You just said you wanted the money..."

"I want you to consider giving the money to your husband's victims..."

"You motherfucker!!   You want me to pay Lina!!"

"Yes..."

"Unfuckin' believable!!   I knew you hadn't changed!! I'm not paying you, Lina, or anybody else a fuckin' dime!! Fuck you!!"

"If you don't give up the money that was awarded to your husband's estate – you can be sued. Lina will join the class action suit the other women are filing..." he lied. "You'll be in court for months. Even if you settle out of court – you'll pay out a lot more than $60,000..."

"$60,000?!   What the hell!!" Jake didn't respond. He just sat there quiet. He knew he had her right where he wanted her... "You're the one that posted his bail..."

"That's not true..."

"I went down there to bail him out and they told me somebody already bailed him out... it all makes sense..."

"Ava – I didn't bail your husband out..."

"You posted his bail to get him out so you could have him killed... and now that he's dead... you want your money..."

"That's not true..."

"I'm calling the police..."

"If that's what you want to do Ava – go ahead..." he said as he got up to leave...

"You're leaving? I thought you wanted the money..."

"Never mind – it's not worth it – I won't bother you again..." he said as he left...

"What the fuck just happened..." she sighed...

"Gotcha!!" Jake exclaimed as he drove off...

CHAPTER 31

"What's this?" Leonard asked as Jake handed him the Lakers Request Form for Dash Board Messages, filled out...

CONGRATULATIONS
BRI & LEONARD

CONGRATULATIONS
LINA & MAGIC

"I want us to propose to our ladies at the first pre-season game in October..."

"Hmmm – October 3rd is on a Monday..."

"Yes it is..."

"That's a great way to start the week..."

"Yes it is..."

"There's just one problem..."

"What's that?"

"They don't post marriage proposals..."

"I thought about that – and I have an idea..."

"What's your idea?"

"We propose to them before the game... They congratulate us at the game..."

"Why do we need this form then?"

"We propose to them, they say yes, we fill out the form, we scan it before we send it. After we send it, we print it out and frame it. We take them to the game. After we get married, we give the framed form to them on our honeymoon..."

"Aww damn – you're in love!!"

"So are you!!"

"I'm happy for us man..." Leonard sighed as he gave Jake a half-hug...

"I'm happy for us too..."

"So where are we getting married?"

"I want to get married in Morocco..."

"Where?"

"Lina's from Morocco. I want to give her a Moroccan wedding to honor her parents and their traditions..."

"Umm... where does that leave us?"

"I don't expect you to get married in Morocco..." Jake laughed... "But you and Bri are family and I know Lina will want you there as much as I do..."

"I'm going to marry Bri in paradise..."

"In paradise?"

"At the Atlantis – Paradise Island, Bahamas..."

"Nice..."

"I've always wanted to be able to say I was married in Paradise..."

"Bri's going to love that..."

"I hope so..." Leonard sighed...

"She will..."

"I have a question..."

"Go ahead..."

"Who's getting married first?"

"You are..."

"Why me?"

"Why not you?"

"How 'bout this – how 'bout you get married first?"

"Why me?"

"We'll go to Morocco for your wedding. After you get married, we'll go to the Bahamas for my wedding – and we'll all honeymoon in Paradise..."

"Our wives will love that..." Jake sighed...

"I have another question..."

"Go ahead..."

"Where are we taking them to celebrate?"

"It won't be El Cholo or Elevate..."

"So where are we going to take them then?"

"I'll make reservations for us at Fleming Steak House..."

"Nice..."

"Thanks – I thought it would be a good idea because it's right across the street from the Staples Center..."

"It's a great idea..."

"Okay – I'll get the tickets now..." Jake said as he sat down at the table and pulled out his laptop...

"They have them on sale already?"

"They went on sale yesterday..."

"You've been watching the site..."

"I had them send an alert to my email..." Jake explained as he ordered the four tickets... "Now all we need to do is fill out these forms, give them our credit cards, and send them off..."

"I like how easy it is to do this..."

"So do I..."

"Where's your printer?"

"It's in my office – I'll send the link to you in your email so can print it, fill it out, scan it, and send it after you get home..."

"Aiight – I'm out..." Leonard said as he went out the door...

"Lieutenant?"

"Yes Tippet?"

"Mrs. Shannon is here to see you..."

"Where is she?"

"She's in your office..."

"Thanks..." Lieutenant Fox said as he went into his office... "Mrs. Shannon – I'm so sorry for your loss..."

"Thank you..." she sighed...

"What can I do for you?"

"Would you make sure they get these?" she asked as she handed Lieutenant Fox three envelopes..."

"What's this?" he asked...

"I would've mailed them myself – but I don't know their addresses – and I don't wanna know them..."

"What is this?"

"Money from my husband's estate..."

"Mrs. Shannon – you don't owe them anything..."

"I don't – but my husband does – and he's dead so..."

"Are you sure you want to do this?"

"I'm sure..."

"Okay – I'll make sure they get it..."

"Thanks..." she said as she got up to leave...

"Mrs. Shannon?"

"Yes Lieutenant?"

"If you ever need anything..."

"I won't..." she interrupted as she left the precinct...

THE PROPOSAL

"Yo!" Jake answered...

"You got the tickets?" Leonard asked...

"Yea..."

"You sure you're ready to do this?"

"I'm the one that should be asking you that..." Jake laughed...

"You're right..."

"You're not having second thoughts – are you?"

"It's not that..."

"What is it then?"

"It just hit me..."

"What?"

"I finally found the one..."

"Yes – you finally found the one..."

"I spent a long time going from woman to woman..."

"We both did...

"And now we're here..."

"Yes we are..."

"I'm about to pull up in front of Bri's now..."

"I'm right behind you..."
"Congratulations Magic..."
"Congratulations Len..."

"Hey..." Bri sighed as she opened the door...

"Hey..." Leonard breathed as he pulled her into a kiss and kissed her passionately...

"Wow..." she breathed...

"C'mon – I have something I need to ask you..." he said as he closed the door, took Bri's hand, and pulled her into the living room...

"Bri..."
"Yes Len?"

"Ever since my parents renewed their vows, I've always said I want to be married in paradise..." he said as he bent down on one knee and opened the ring box... "Will you marry me in the Atlantis, Paradise Island, Bahamas?"

"I'd love to marry you in Paradise..."

"Is that a yes?"

"Yes Len – Yes – I'll marry you in Paradise..." Leonard put the ring on her finder and before he could get up off his knee, Bri knelt down in front of him, pulled him into a kiss, pushed him down, and straddled him...

"We're going to be late for the game..." he panted...

"I'll make this quick..." she panted as she moved down between his legs...

"Hey..." Lina sighed as she opened the door. Jake went inside, closed the door, pulled Lina into his arms, and kissed her so hard it startled her...

"Magic... What..." Jake kissed her again and Lina began to relax...

"C'mon..." he said as he took her by the hand and led her into the living room...

"Lina?"

"Yes Magic?"

"I know you're your father's Moroccan Princess..." he said as he got down on one knee and opened the ring box... "But I want to know if you'll be my Moroccan Princess..."

"Oh Magic..." Lina whispered as she started crying...

"Will you marry me?"

"Yes Magic... Yes..." Jake put the ring on her finger, stood up, picked her up off the floor, kissed her hard, and put her back down...

"Are you ready to go to the game?"

"Yes..."

"This is Gayle Anderson, News Anchor, KTLA5 News. We interrupt our regularly scheduled programming to bring you an announcement. Two couples have just confirmed their engagement outside the Staples Center. KTLAT is live outside the Staples Center now - go ahead Ellina...

"We're engaged!!" Lina and Bri both blurted out in unison when they saw each other... "Oh my God – Congratulations!!" they both exclaimed in unison as they hugged each other and cried...

"Congratulations..." Leonard and Jake said in unison as they hugged...

"This is Ellina Abovian, Reporter, KTLA5 News. I'm here outside the Staples Center. So which one of you planned this?" Ellina asked as she walked up to them...

"We both did..." Jake answered...

"Have you set a date?"

"We just got engaged..." Leonard laughed...

"Let's introduce the happy couples to our viewers..." she said as she gave Jake the microphone...

"I'm Jake Thompson and this is my fiancée, Lina..." he said as he pulled Lina close to him and kissed her. Everyone outside applauded as he passed the microphone to Leonard...

"I'm Leonard Allen and this is my fiancée Bri..." he said as he pulled Bri close to him and kissed her. Everyone outside applauded as he passed the microphone back to Ellina...

"Love is in the air tonight - back to you Gayle..."

"This is Gayle Anderson, News Anchor, KTLA5 News. KTLA5 is happy to congratulate you on your engagements. We now return to our regularly scheduled programming..."

"How did they know we'd be here?" Leonard asked...

"I called them..." Jake answered as they went inside to their seats...

"Who are the Lakers playing tonight?" Bri asked...

"The Kings..." Lina answered...

"Ladies – look..." Leonard said as he pointed to the DASH Boards between suite levels A & B...

"Oh my God!!" they both exclaimed as they both pulled their finances into a kiss...

"How did you do that?" Lina asked...

"It's easy – you fill out the form, you give them the date, they run it..." Jake answered...

"I love you so much!!" Lina exclaimed as she pulled him into another kiss...

"Are you going to let him watch the game?" Leonard laughed...

"Maybe not!" Bri laughed as she pulled Leonard into a kiss...

"Oh no – look what we started!!" Leonard laughed...

"This is just the beginning..." Jake sighed as he pulled Lina into a kiss. The game went on but the four of them were acting as if they were attending their private engagement party instead of a pre-season game. Every time Kobe Bryant or Pau Gasol scored, the crowd cheered and they would all kiss...

"Where are we going now?" Bri asked as they finally got up to leave...

"You'll see..." Jake answered...

"Welcome to Fleming Steak House – do you have a reservation?" the hostess asked...

"Jake Thompson – party of four..." Jake answered...

"Yes Sir Mr. Thompson – come with me..." the hostess instructed as they followed him into a private dining room...

"We have the room to ourselves?" Bri asked...

"Yes..." Leonard answered...

"I love you..."

"I love you too Mrs. Allen..." he breathed as he pulled her into a kiss...

"I can't wait to be Mrs. Thompson..." Lina sighed...

"You won't be waiting long..." Jake breathed as he pulled her into a kiss...

"Good evening – and congratulations..." the waiter said as he brought over the menus...

"Thank you..." they all said in unison...

"Can I start you off with Acqua Panna or San Pellegrino?"

"San Pellegrino!!" they all exclaimed in unison...

"Okay – for appetizers we have Crab Cake Bites, Fleming's Tots, Filet & Mushroom Puff Pastry, Chicken Satay, Shrimp Cocktail, Prosciutto-Wrapped Shrimp, Chicpea & Eggplant Bites, Prime Meatballs, and Sweet & Spicy Filet Skewers..."

"All of them!!" Bri exclaimed...

"Very well – I'll put in the order for your appetizers and then I'll be back with your drinks..." the waiter said as he went to place their order...

"I have a question..." Lina said...

"Yes Lina?" Jake answered...

"Who's getting married first?"

"We are..."

"Oh thank God – I thought you wanted to do a double wedding!!" Bri laughed...

"You wouldn't like a double wedding?" Leonard asked...

"Well... no..."

"Me either!!" Lina exclaimed...

"Well – I guess we should tell them..." Jake suggested...

"You planned our wedding?!" Lina exclaimed...

"We didn't plan our weddings – but we have a plan..." Leonard answered...

"What's the plan – we wanna know!!" Bri exclaimed...

"Here are your drinks..." the waiter said as he put them on the table... "Have you had a chance to look at the menu?"

"Not yet..." Jake answered...

"I'll be back in a few minutes..." the waiter said as he went to go check on the appetizers...

"Everyone pick up your glass..." Jake said as he raised his glass... "Here's to the future couples – the Thompson's and the Allen's..."

"Here's to the Thompson's and the Allen's..." they all repeated as they clinked their glasses and took a sip...

"Okay – what's the plan?" Bri asked...

"Look at the menu, pick out what you want..." Leonard said...

"I wanna know what the plan is..." Bri whined...

"And you will..." Leonard breathed as he kissed her...

"Okay..." she sighed...

"I don't think I'll have room for salad..." Lina said...

"We're going to be here for a while..." Jake said...

"The Chopped Wedge Salad looks good..." Bri said...

"Let's go with that..." Leonard said...

"Sounds good to me..." Jake agreed...

"I don't want any snacks..." Lina said...

"I don't either..." Bri agreed...

"I'm looking at the Barbecue Scottish Salmon Fillet..." Leonard said...

"I'll get the Roasted Beef Tenderloin..." Bri said...

"I'll get the Double Breast of Chicken..." Lina said...

"I'll get the Main Filet Mignon..." Jake said...

"And your sides?' the waiter asked. They all laughed because they didn't realize the waiter was standing there...

"I'll have the Roasted Asparagus..." Leonard said...

"I'll have the North Atlantic Lobster Macaroni & Cheese..." Lina said...

"I'll have the Crispy Brussel Sprouts & Bacon..." Bri said...

"I'll have the Fleming's Potatoes..." Jake said...

"Got it – here are your appetizers..." the waiter said as he put them on the table... "I'll go place your orders, I'll wait until you're finished with your appetizers, and then I'll bring out your salad..." he said before he went to place their order...

"Can you tell us the plan now? Please?" Bri asked as she put her hand between Leonard's legs...

"You keep that up and I'll knock all this food on the floor and do you right here..."

"Okay – Okay – I'll stop!!" Bri laughed...

"I dare you!!" Jake laughed...

"I don't dare you!!" Lina laughed... "I'm hungry!!"

"Okay – here's what we wanna do – we wanna go to Morocco first..." Jake answered...

"Oh Magic!!" Lina exclaimed as she started crying...

"You and I will get married there. Len and Bri will be in our wedding..."

"Yes Magic... yes..."

"We'll go from Morocco to the Atlantis in Paradise Island..." Leonard added... "Magic and Lina will be in our wedding. After we get married, we'll all honeymoon in Paradise..."

"Oh Len... I love it..." Bri said as she started crying...

"I can't wait to plan our wedding..."Lina said...

"What's a Moroccan wedding like?" Bri asked...

"It takes about a week..." Lina answered...

"A week?!" Bri exclaimed...

"Yes – I'll go over everything when you come over..."

"Sounds like I'm taking a month off work..." Bri laughed...

"You probably won't be there much longer..." Leonard said...

"Did you plan our dates too?" Lina asked...

"No..." Jake answered as they continued eating...

"Here's your salad..." the waiter said as he brought the salad to the tale...

"I thought he was going to wait until we were finished..." Leonard laughed...

"I guess not..." Jake laughed...

"I can't believe I'm getting married in Morocco..."Lina sighed...

"I can't wait to meet your family..." Bri sighed...

"My mother's going to love you..."

"This'll be a first for me..."Leonard said...

"It'll be a first for all of us..." Jake said as they continued eating...

"Here are your entrees..." the waiter said as he put their food on the table... "Have you had a chance to look at the dessert menu?"

"We'll take the chocolate covered strawberries..." Jake answered...

"I'll be back with your dessert..."

"I'm feeling a way about him rushing us!!" Leonard laughed...

"Don't take it personal – he just wants us to get our food before the kitchen closes..." Jake laughed...

"I can't wait for us to get home..." Bri sighed...

"Me either..." Lina sighed...

"Let's hurry up and make that happen..." Leonard said as he fed Bri a strawberry. Bri picked up a strawberry and fed it to Leonard as Jake fed Lina a strawberry. Lina picked up a strawberry, put it in her mouth, and pulled Jake into a kiss...

"Aww shit – that's what I'm talkin' about!!" Bri exclaimed as she did the same thing with Leonard. They were all oblivious to the waiter as he put the check on the table...

"Common – let's go home..."Leonard said as he led Bri out the restaurant to the car...

"C'mon..." Jake said as he led Lina out the restaurant to the car...

"I'll call you..." Leonard said as he drove off...

"Magic?"

"Yes Lina?"

"Can you take me home?"

"That was the plan..."

"I mean my apartment..."

"You sure?"

"Yea..."

"Okay – if that's what you want..." he sighed. Lina knew he was disappointed but what he didn't know was that she had a surprise for him... "We're here..." he sighed...

"Can you come upstairs? I need your held with something..."

"Sure..." he answered as he locked the car and followed her upstairs. Lina unlocked the door and pulled him inside... "What do you need help with?"

"Packing..."

"You wanna pack for the honeymoon already?" he laughed...

"No Magic... I need you to help me pack because I'm moving out... and I'm moving in... With you..." Jake pulled her into a kiss and kissed her hard...

"Where do we start?'

"In the bedroom..." she answered as she took him by the hand and pulled him towards the bedroom...

"Lieutenant..."

"Yes?"

"There's a private call for you on line one..." Captain Tippet said...

"Do we know where the call is from?"

"He has an accent – he said you'll know who it is..."

"Okay – thanks..." Lieutenant Fox went into his office and closed the door... "This is Lieutenant Fox..."

"Hello Robert..."

"You have the wrong number..." Lieutenant Fox hung up the desk phone, took out his private cell phone, and called Lina's father..."

"Hello Lieutenant – How are you?"

"Why the hell would you call my desk phone?"

"I knew that would get your attention..."

"You had my attention!!"

"If I had your attention, you would've called me..."

"I'm sorry I haven't called you sooner – I had to do my job – or at least make it look I was doing my job..."

"And have you done your job?"

"Absolutely..."

"So my daughter is safe?"

"Your daughter is safe..."

"This Magic Man – is he a good man?"

"His father was a good man..."

"I didn't ask you about his father..."

"He's a lot like you..."

"What does that mean?"

"He'll do anything to protect your daughter..."

"Does my daughter have anything to worry about?"

"Not that I can tell..."

"So... from what you **CAN** tell... Did this Magic Man kill him?"

"Not that I can tell..."

"I'm very happy to hear that..."

"Oh my God..."

"That would be Allah... Not me..."

"It was you..."

"I have no idea what you're talking about..."

"You bailed him out..."

"It's been a pleasure catching up Lieutenant..." Youssef said as he hung up...

www.ingramcontent.com/pod-product-compliance
Lightning Source LLC
Chambersburg PA
CBHW051145030726
47504CB00004B/1055

* 9 7 9 8 9 8 5 5 2 9 0 5 0 *